Owens, Iris
   Hope Diamond Refuses.

ALSO BY IRIS OWENS
After Claude

Hope Diamond
Refuses

Hope Diamond Refuses

A NOVEL BY

IRIS OWENS

ALFRED A. KNOPF · NEW YORK · 1984

THIS IS A BORZOI BOOK

PUBLISHED BY

ALFRED A. KNOPF, INC.

Published in the United States by
Alfred A. Knopf, Inc., New York,
and simultaneously in Canada by
Random House of Canada Limited, Toronto.
Distributed by Random House, Inc., New York.
Library of Congress
Cataloging in Publication Data
Owens, Iris.   Hope Diamond refuses.
I. Title.
PS3554.A3H6   1984   813'.54   83-48886
ISBN 0-394-51830-6
Manufactured in the United States of America
First Edition

\

For William F. Klein

ACKNOWLEDGMENTS

It gives me pleasure to express my gratitude for the support and aid received from Paula Landesman, Knight Landesman, Leon Friedman, Victoria Wilson, Sandro Bocala, the Yaddo Colony, the MacDowell Colony, the Creative Artists Public Service Program, the Author's League, and most particularly to Joellyn Ausanka whose assistance to me was a gift beyond measure.

1

I could hardly wait for Leo Hermann to arrive in order to get rid of him. I was finished with the piker, and though I had no desire to see him, there were a couple of statements I preferred to make in person. I'd been refining and rehearsing my farewell address since he'd called from Kennedy to jubilantly announce his return, safe and sound, from a three-week safari in darkest Africa, of all places to convey his agoraphobic wife. In all fairness, it was Madame Hermann who insisted on the expedition, as she was compensating for twelve long years of being locked behind the guarded doors of their Central Park West fortress, which really, despite all the hand wringing, suited Leo like nobody's business. To have Mama confined to the house, eagerly awaiting her darling's reports on the state of the world? It was perfect! And just when everyone in the Hermann family—Leo, the Crazy, and their twelve-year-old offspring, Cynthia, whose belated birth marked the onset of her mother's phobia—had adjusted to the situation, along came a new-style therapy, and in no time flat Muriel had confronted her fears and was out on the homicidal streets, hankering for wild beasts, guns, and a jungle or two to conquer.

Naturally, my soon-to-be-former lover expressed joy at his wife's miraculous recovery. "She deserves her chance to live," Leo decreed, just as benign as God is supposed to be. In principle, Muriel had received very little coverage on my beat, but Leo could not resist commenting on her rapid strides toward mental health. Overnight this housebound woman I'd never met was sufficiently stable to lead her very own pack of anxiety-ridden neurotics to Bloomingdale's, then Zabar's; she even took ten of the severest cases to Leopold's, Leo's celebrity haunt on West Forty-ninth Street. Leo was elated that not one of her group had gone berserk, wrecked his restaurant, or died of a panic attack. Anyway, my decision had nothing to do with his wife, who was welcome to Leo's undivided services. It had entirely to do with her husband, who was, one, cheap; two, old; and three, indescribably mediocre. Otherwise he was an enchanting human being, as well as a decorated hero of a minor war.

"Leo," I was planning to say, "the Geneva Convention has outlawed white slavery, so tell me, what are you doing here?" That one line, in my opinion, summed up the terms of our bargain-basement affair. It made no sense that such a nonentity should feel entitled to my time and energy without once bringing me a memento that couldn't be eliminated through my digestive tract! "Leo," I was then planning to say, "what do you take me for, a fantasy, a walking dream, a genie who curls up inside a lamp and lives off kerosene when you're not here violating me?" A person didn't have to be a genius to look at my crummy setup and figure out any number of ways in which to pay me homage.

I was genuinely curious to hear what the man would say in his own defense. How could he possibly refute my charges? Did it seem normal to him for someone of my caliber to be stuck down here on Grove Street in a single room—one and a half rooms, counting the kitchen foyer—of a dark, stuffy garden apartment? This particular garden apartment didn't even bother to have a rear door leading out to the garden planted in my landlady Libby Straus's fertile imagination. There was space back there, in the neglected courtyard, for an Eden, but that domain could be entered only by an exterior stairway attached to the parlor floor directly overhead, which was left perpetually vacant by Libby's younger brother, Stuart, who was cohabiting on the Cape with a poet–window washer called Gregory, the celebrated author of a gravely embarrassing book of verse enti-tled *Pane*. Libby and Stuart, the Straus heirs, had inherited this brownstone, a hellhole of hazards, from their late playboy fa-ther, who used the premises as a secret love nest that got fur-nished and decorated by a fast-changing procession of frisky dancing girls. The more lurid of the trappings ended up stashed in the dungeon it is my good fortune to occupy.

The blast of the front doorbell signaled that the curtain was about to go up on my grand finale. I reached for the last Van-tage in the crumpled pack and lay back on my foam rubber bier, cunningly concealed behind a four-panel geisha screen, as I had no objections to the image of Leo panting at my closed door, wondering why I wasn't running out to welcome the next bout of exploitation. A second piercing ring of the bell practically threw me to the bedside prayer rug.

I headed for the barred windows and bolted door located in the front foyer. I raised a corner of the bamboo blind that af-fords me some but not much privacy and, by craning my neck while spiraling my spine, checked to make sure the caller was Leo and not some dehydrated Moonie soliciting a blood trans-fusion. Not for me the ease of pressing a button and inquiring who is there. I am obliged to fling open the shades and expose myself to every beggar and bum who careens off Sheridan Square to make a comfort station of the shallow well that sepa-rates me from the sidewalk. Leo Hermann adores my life-style; it's everything debased he ever dreamed of before he married Muriel, who was, after all, entitled to the comforts due a de-voted wife and mother.

I peered out the window, as Gregory wrote in one of his masterpieces—except he was referring to his birth trauma—and saw with some consternation it wasn't Leo cooling his heels. There, skinny as the spikes of the wrought-iron gates that so enhance her property—a historical landmark, if plaques do not lie—stood my landlady, Libby Straus, revealed by more daylight

than I personally prefer. Of late, my trimmed-down landlady
has taken to wearing the floral rayon dress in which Stella Dal-
las had the good sense not to attend her daughter's wedding.
From top to toe, from a frizzy, hennaed permanent she has only
to wash and let dry on her head like rope down to an assem-
blage of battered shopping bags and open-toed wedgies, the
humbly attired heiress is able to blend nicely with the army of
freaks who have occupied the streets of Manhattan. Of course,
she can afford to parade around in rags since she is rich, chroni-
cally, congenitally rich, so rich her central fixation is the awful
possibility that humanity might be more interested in her tons
of money than in her vivacious personality.

By the time I let her in, Libby was hyperventilating with re-
pressed rage, as it is a canon of her current credo to transcend
negativity. Libby of the sunken eyes and haughty mien is
learning to love.

"Hello, Hope." She brushed by me with a frigid smile and
went straight for the counter that borders a triumph of rust
and dripping faucets ingeniously tagged an efficiency kitchen.
"Put up beaded curtains" has been my landlady's response to
my objections over this eyesore that is the first shock to assault
anyone crossing my threshold. She also made the brilliant suggestion that I hang beads in the square archway separating the
entrance foyer from the windowless inner sanctum, as if this
overstuffed crypt could use yet another touch of exotica. It's no
fun for me to explain to all newcomers that none of this—not
the oxblood carpeting, not the yellowing, marbleized walls, not
the oversized cushion couch or the velour easy chairs or a single
one of the rare knickknacks crammed onto a black marble slab
of a table the builders of Stonehenge couldn't budge—none of
it is mine, lest the interloper identify me with my surroundings. "I'm not disturbing you or anything, am I?" Libby asked
in her wispy finishing-school voice.

"Not yet," I said, and watched as she deposited her armloads of shopping bags on the milk-glass countertop. Out of these burgeoning bags, I suppose I might mention, has magically appeared the bulk of my wardrobe as bestowed on me by the gracious shopping fairy, a.k.a. Libby Straus. The amazing shrinking heiress has a disturbed self-image, especially in Bendel's, and most of her ticketed, brand-new "mistakes" end up crushed into the antique mirrored wardrobe that presides over the entrance foyer.

"I have the most incredible news for you," she breathlessly informed me, sliding her emaciated form onto one of the wicker-backed barstools at the counter.

"Don't make yourself too comfortable," I warned her. "I'm expecting someone soon." I did not go into specifics because Leo does not find favor with my landlady, who has more reasons for eliminating men from the running than the Germans did from their celebrated Olympics.

"Not too soon," she protested, digging into the burlap tote hanging off her stick arm to extract a box of fancy Nat Shermans. My landlady may have her prohibitions, virtually countless, but she indulges in her forty to fifty smokes per diem. It was that, she claimed, or donate her bloated remains to the Häagen Dazs Foundation.

"Very soon," I corrected her as I eased my way to the counter. "In fact, there's hardly time for us to finish our cigarettes before I'm afraid I'll have to ask you to leave."

"But, Hope, I must tell you my news." She gave me a light with a click of her disposable lighter. The tiny mirrors on the bodice of my caftan ignited in Libby's tinted lenses. She was quite a sight, with that stiff mop of hair, her rimless sunglasses, and her bright red glossy lips.

"You'll have to tell me later," I said with finality.

Libby flicked a nonexistent ash into the gaping jaws of my one-of-a-kind crocodile ashtray and studied me briefly before sending her shielded eyes on a rapid mine-detecting tour of my gloomy quarters, her search hesitating, as it invariably does, at the geisha screen, which is falling apart but manages to serve its purpose.

"Why do you keep it so dark back there?" she said in a huffy tone, supporting herself on the bottom rung of the stool and stretching out to her full five feet ten inches of rayon-draped bones to get a clearer view of the temptations within. Like most people who conduct their love lives primarily in the head, my landlady is convinced the rest of mankind is engaged in a nonstop orgy that takes cover when she makes an entrance. "There's nobody back there, is there?" she asked, swaying in the direction of her suspicious gaze.

"No," I said, "of course not."

She sniffed the dim air. "It's awful, Hope, the way you stagnate in here with the blinds down and those silly pink lampshades you imagine are so flattering and youthful, as if you really had to be concerned with age." She settled into her chair, but it would be a mistake to say she settled in with an air of satisfaction. "That new friend of yours—what's his name, Rush? He's always here, isn't he?"

"Libby," I said, "I'm alone, but not as alone as I wish to be."

I was coming to the end of my fathomless tolerance for the human condition, which my landlady sensed with a sly inward smile. Since her love conversion she has adopted an array of furtive smiles, like secret kisses she is blowing to herself.

"How long do we have before he gets back?" She peeled off her glasses and scrutinized me with eyes sunk in rings Saturn would envy.

"Before who gets back?" I pleaded for mercy. I was sorry I'd ever alluded to Rush, a sportswriter I'd lured out of Leo's establishment the very night the great white hunter vanished into the bush. I forgot for a frivolous moment how Libby's fantasies focus on my meager existence, since if mortal man so much as breathes on the girl, she spends the following week crouched in her gynecologist's office.

"Guess who I had lunch with today," she persisted. She was vibrating with an excitement that failed to impress me, as excitement comes with the cadaverous package.

"Your embalmer?" I ventured. Libby laughed at my witticism. There are two Libbys I've had to contend with, a skinny one and a fat one, and except for the fact that both are filthy rich and neither gets laid, they are sufficiently dissimilar to qualify her as a multiple personality. It's the skinny manic one Libby has taken to be her virgin bride, and words can't describe how she caters to her beloved. There are gurus and acupuncturists and shiatsu massages and exercise classes and shopping sprees and Broadway shows—she's on the town from morning till night, unlike the fat depressive who got banished to the top-floor duplex of the Grove Street mansion, a pity, really, since Fat Libby was easily the prettier of the team, with her acres of milky skin, baby-fine reddish hair, green eyes, and a sullen air of subdued sexuality, plus, admittedly, those Godzilla thighs and a behind as ample as her bank account.

"Don't guess, don't even try to guess." She let me off the hook, her eyes sending out unreadable signals. "I'll tell you if you'll make me a cup of coffee."

"Libby," I cried, "you're not listening to me. I'm not getting through to you. Is starvation damaging your senses?"

"Starvation." She chuckled softly and crossed her fleshless thighs. "I'm far from starvation. I'm actually at my ideal weight."

"Ideal for what, levitating?" I sat on the adjoining stool and impulsively counseled her. "Libby," I said, "there's a limit to thin, and you've passed it. You'd better start eating solid food before you die."

She sucked in her hollow and rouged cheeks and bristled. "I eat quite enough, and I feel marvelous. I've never had more energy, and now that I've finally attained my ideal weight, I will not be influenced by a pack of saboteurs who for some hostile reason prefer me fat." She waved me off with a flourish of her freshly lit cigarette.

"Terrific. So you're ideal. Is that your incredible news that can't wait?"

Libby laughed. A sound poignant as a sob rose from her famished interior.

"Not quite." She nervously swallowed air. I suppose I should have suspected something serious was in the works, but I was primarily concerned with getting her out before Leo arrived for the last of his cameo appearances.

"Okay, Libby," I relented, "talk, but make it fast."

"Promise me you won't get hysterical," she said, and her words filled me with a vague panic. She took a deep breath. "Someone very special arrived at Kennedy Airport this morning who is dying to see you."

It took awhile for her words to sink in. I stared at her. She couldn't possibly be making this fuss over Leo Hermann. Or could she? How follow the workings of her malnourished brain?

"You're not talking about Leo Hermann, are you, Libby?"

"Leo Hermann? Leo Hermann?" she repeated with an emphasis bordering on disgust. "Is he back? Is that who you're waiting for? Hope, really!"

That was all I needed, a lecture from her on how to conduct my private life.

"Who's dying to see me, Libby?" I said.

And then, without a pause, she let me have it. "Joanne," she softly discharged.

"Who?" My mouth went dry, parched, a Red Sea opening along my esophagus.

"You heard me," Libby answered, inching toward the door. Of course, she was right.

Joanne. The name scorched my heart.

"Joanne is in New York?" My ears were ringing. I clung dizzily to the edge of the counter.

"I assume so, unless she caught a return flight to Ustan right after lunch."

"Don't you dare be sarcastic with me, you idiot!" I yelled.

Libby tensed her giant insect body. "I will not stay here and listen to your insults!" *Now* she was leaving! Hit men hung around their dirty work longer.

"Don't leave, please." I pulled at one of her shopping bags. "Excuse me. It was just the shock. Joanne in America. Libby, we have to talk."

"We'll talk later. I don't want to run into Leo." She stayed at a safe distance, rigid and ready as a karate contender.

"Forget about Leo," I told her. "Who cares about Leo?" Leo who? Leo had been wiped from my mind like a piece of irrelevant fiction. Joanne was my crushing reality.

"But he might be here any minute." Libby relaxed her defensive stance. I could tell she knew the worst of it was over. Her attitude conveyed the relief she was feeling to have survived her perilous mission.

"I was afraid you'd overreact and make a scene," she said in the haughty tones she employs to maintain her network of loving relationships.

"How long have you known she was coming?" I knew those two false friends kept up a sporadic correspondence.

"I swear to you, Hope, it was a complete surprise to me. She said she flew over on an impulse."

An impulse! I did not permit myself to dwell on the jetting impulses my successor could gratify while I could hardly scrounge up the taxi fare to the airport. I used all of my inner resources to hold Libby there in hypnotic passivity.

"Why is she here? What is she doing here?"

"I don't know," she impatiently responded. "She is *still* an American, even if she is a princess in Ustan."

I winced at Libby's attack of patriotism.

"Is she alone?" It was not an easy question for me to ask.

"She's not with Babi, if that's what's worrying you."

I took my first free breath. My lungs ached. My rib cage ached.

"If you're willing," Libby condescended, "I'd be glad to have a cup of coffee."

"My pleasure," I said, and stood there, blocking the exit, until she'd reseated herself at the counter. I made a dash for the sink to fill the copper kettle before my customer could cancel her order. Libby observed me closely, nervously tapping her red-tipped talons on the milk-glass countertop. I tore open a fresh package of Oreos and shoved one of the chocolate resuscitators onto my tongue. My blood sugar had plummeted to coma level. I dropped the bag of cookies on the counter, where they captured Libby's avid attention.

"Have one," I snapped at her.

"Oh, no, I couldn't possibly. I had a huge lunch." She rubbed her concavity.

"I bet," I said.

She tore her eyes away from the temptation. "I was almost as bowled over as you are when Joanne called this morning." Libby lit up a cigarette as she began her report. "At first I didn't even recognize her voice. How long has it been? Over five years?"

I nodded to keep her talking. I dealt two shallow terra-cotta bowls onto the counter. I unscrewed the economy-sized jar of Nescafé. I tossed a couple of teaspoons close to the bowls. My gestures were mechanical. Automatic. It felt as though I were observing myself in a bad dream.

"She'd just checked into a hotel in the East Sixties, one I've never heard of, and she begged me to meet her for lunch."

That hateful word again.

"Of course, I was dying to see her, and we made a twelve o'clock date at the Ginger Man. Honestly, Hope, if she hadn't called and we hadn't made a definite appointment and I wasn't there looking for her, I would never in a million years have recognized Joanne. You think I'm thin? You should see her. She must be a size two, tops."

You can't be too rich or too thin, I grimly recited to myself.

"And frankly," Libby's breathtaking monologue continued, "I didn't find it at all becoming. It might have been the ravages of jet lag—it's a sixteen- or seventeen-hour flight from Ustan—but she really didn't look well, not at all like the vibrant, energetic Joanne I used to know. The dress she was wearing, a really rancid green, didn't help the matter." One of those adorable smiles wafted across her melancholy features as she drifted into a private reverie.

"Libby, keep talking!" I jolted her out of the beauty contest parading through her head.

She bestirred herself, crossing and uncrossing her twig legs. "Of course, we were both overwhelmed to see each other after all these years. Joanne was flabbergasted at my transformation. I guess she's never really seen me at my ideal weight, and we both ordered the spinach salad, delicious even without the fattening dressing, and Joanne had hers without bacon, she still doesn't eat red meat—"

"Libby," I screamed, "I am not interested in what the calculating bitch ate unless she choked on it!"

My landlady's plucked brows lifted to the edges of her mangled hairline. "That's a terribly hostile thing to say."

"Forgive me." My heart was beating at a staccato pace. "Forgive my hostility. Somehow I still harbor feelings of hostility toward the bitch who eloped with my husband."

"Your husband," she affectionately mocked me. "What kind of husband was Babi to you? You didn't live with him. You weren't lovers any more. My God, you were always throwing him out. No one knew you two were married until you had to get divorced."

It was precisely the ignorant and insensitive response I'd expected. "I knew we were married." I leaned closer and addressed her with heroic restraint. "Babi knew we were married. We were married, Libby, good and married."

"You had a marriage license, if that's what you mean." She propped herself up on her dagger elbows. "The point I'm making is you never told me you were married, and Joanne certainly didn't know till much later, so you have absolutely no right to be hostile toward her." She straightened up her drooping torso and dropped her shadowed lids. "I was in love with him. She was my best friend. If anyone was hurt, it was me." She bounced a loose fist off her corrugated chest.

"Fine," I said, "agreed. You were the injured party. You were the one who lost him. You were the one who was betrayed. Is that why you were so overwhelmed to see your enemy again?"

"But that's all ancient history. How long can you hold a grudge?" It took her a moment to contort her big red mouth into a tender smile. "Joanne showed me snapshots of her little boy. Such a darling. Big black eyes and a mass of black curls, just like his daddy. Wait till you see him, he's to die." Libby paused to reflect on the pleasure awaiting me. What wouldn't I have given for a few minutes with Fat Libby, who made no pretense of forgiving Joanne? Unfortunately, that entity had long since been swallowed and digested by this lean and false serpent.

"Where the hell is Leo?" I said, storming out from behind the counter to lift one of the window blinds. It made me sick to think of being hounded by all these people I wished I'd never met.

Libby took rapid, ladylike sips of her steaming coffee. "I guess I'd better get moving. What time was he supposed to get here?" She pushed the bowl aside with a distasteful expression and pressed the stem of the pulsar watch strapped to her spindly wrist.

"He wasn't sure." I let the blind drop back into place.

"He never is, is he?" she said sweetly, and then something in my face made her change her tune. "He was probably held up at customs," she said with elaborate tact.

"Held up for what? The valuable gems he was smuggling in for me?"

"Please"—she lifted her stick arms in mock defense—"let's not get on the subject of the gifts you never got. That's the least of what that man never gave you. So"—she moved the conference along—"can I tell Joanne our lunch is on for to-morrow?"

"You can tell her anything you want, but I have no intention of seeing her."

Libby released a tiny shriek. "You *have* to see her. What excuse do you have for not seeing her? Joanne doesn't know after all these years you've decided you were the injured party. It was an amicable enough divorce, considering the rancorous quality of your marriage." Libby was so delighted with her sally she gave herself an Oreo as a reward, taking little mouse bites around the edges and emitting small squeals of pleasure. "It will be fun, the three of us together again. Come on, Hope, don't be difficult. Joanne is dying to see you."

"Why?" I bleakly demanded. "What does she imagine I've been left worth stealing?"

"Don't talk yourself into some nonsensical position. Joanne did not steal Babi from you. She didn't steal him from me either. They met. They were ideally suited. They fell in love and they married. It happens to some fortunate people in this world."

I paced the narrow entryway. "How sweet," I said, "how romantic. What a pretty picture you paint. Why did you leave out the tiny detail of the evil midget being pregnant as a whale when she hooked my husband?"

Libby laughed in spite of herself and covered her lying mouth. Her possum eyes glittered with a secret delight. What would she do without my giving voice to all her forbidden negativity?

"That's really a low blow, Hope. You know very well Joanne did not force Babi to marry her."

"Oh, no. Then explain to me how come they've been legally man and wife four years, maximum, and have a son who is pursuing Shelley Winters."

Libby gave another one of her ladylike shrieks. "That is, without doubt, one of the craziest things I've ever heard you say. Your whole attitude is crazy." She elaborated on the theme. "I told you when their affair started, and you certainly weren't bothered then. I was the one who suffered." Again the proud fist went to her chest.

"I admit, Libby, I was distracted at the time this catastrophe occurred. The whole country was distracted. We were having a revolution! A president was being impeached! Every responsible person was glued to his television set except Joanne, who was busy getting herself knocked up."

Libby sank her face into her palm. "If Joanne could hear this slander you are spouting, she would positively die. All through lunch it was Hope this and Hope that. You know she's always adored you." She split the Oreo apart in a nervous seizure.

You bet I knew. Would I ever recover from Joanne's adoration? Her stirring tribute to my intelligence, my independence, my beauty, my *maturity,* eulogies that dropped like withered carnations into my open grave as she marched into my life at war with male supremacy and the nuclear family and marched out of it a certified wife and mother!

Libby pushed the bag of Oreos out of reach and got to her feet, shaking crumbs from her sleazy skirt.

"You want my sincere opinion, Hope?" She took my arm to arrest my agitated pacing. "You should see Joanne for your own good. It will really cheer you up. I was a bit ambivalent, too, about seeing her, I admit. She'd hurt me, and those wounds are slow to heal. But the important thing is, if you permit them to, they do heal. See her, Hope. It was such a relief to clear my karma with Joanne and to acknowledge that I hadn't been ready for a truly intimate relationship with the prince. Joanne was not to blame. And I also realized something more important: I never would be ready for anyone else until I freed myself from the past. Free yourself, Hope. Don't let these stupid regrets of the past destroy the present."

Could you drown it in insect repellent! There, preaching karma, was the perpetrator of my searing loss. What we both knew, but did not say, was that it was Libby's insane fixation on achieving an ideal fucking weight that had driven my husband into the treacherous arms of her fiendishly fertile friend!

"Did it ever occur to you my present consists of nothing but bills coming in on my past?"

"Which Babi is only too glad to pay," she consoled me.

Glad! The diseases I had to wish on myself to squeeze a few extra pennies out of the billionaire prince of Ustan.

"Libby, this session is over. I have another patient waiting."

"You mean you're actually refusing to join us for lunch?" She stood there, stunned at the social faux pas I was ready to commit.

"I hate lunches! What am I, some suburban housewife who escapes from her misery by lunching with the girls?"

"Then Joanne and I will come down here after lunch." She came up with a quick compromise.

"Here? Here to this scuzzy, disgusting, loathsome cellar? Are you crazy enough to think I'd entertain Princess Joanne here?"

Even as the words leapfrogged from my lips, I knew I'd gone too far. The property owner went wooden with offense and stared at the worn parquet tiles on the foyer floor. We enjoyed a moment's silence, disturbed only by the roar of a rutting motorcycle trying to mount the front stoop.

"You are so ungrateful. Here I let you live in the midst of my father's splendid collection. Everyone who comes here is enchanted by the place." She lifted her eyes so I shouldn't think she was addressing her wedgies. "You haven't even considered paying rent since Babi left America. Yet all you ever do is complain and say how much you hate it here. If you hate it that much, Hope, if it shames you to receive an old friend in this *pied-à-terre* furnished with my family heirlooms, then I advise you to find better accommodations as soon as possible."

She spun around and stamped her way to the door, her shoulder blades jutting through her dress like horns. I grabbed hold of her.

"Libby, can't you take a joke? Really, sometimes I suspect that when you lost all that superfluous flesh, you accidentally lost your fabulous sense of humor. I don't hate it here, I love it. I feel honored to be the custodian of your father's sacred tomb." My face ached from grinning at her. "It's only the prospect of seeing Joanne that made me forget for a minute how much I love my live-in job here."

"Then you will see her." Libby snatched up victory from the ashes of my defeat.

"As long as I can see her here, I can't imagine a single objection. Don't forget the crap you left on the counter," I wearily reminded her. She was always leaving her latest purchases behind.

As she fussed at the counter, the doorbell rang, and of course, it was Leo, his name a bruise on the lips of a royal prince's former consort.

2

Leo stood framed in the doorway, a parcel clutched in his hand. I wouldn't have been particularly happy to see Paul Newman, so Leo, whom some claim he resembles, was hardly a thrill.

"Hiya, pal." He looked straight at me, his eyes sky blue against a recently acquired tan. There was a narrow ridge of bleached skin under his gray, curly hairline, caused, I presumed, by Frank Buck's pith helmet. He was sporting his customary corduroy fatigues, a blue work shirt, and one of his many khaki-colored Windbreakers. When last I'd seen Leo, he'd been of average height, with a stocky build, a large head, and a boyish, sly face, and he looked so familiar it was as if the man had stepped out of my place for a minute to pick up whatever it was he so conspicuously carried. Was it possible that he had remembered to bring his sovereign a tribute?

"Hello, Leo," I said.

He pinned me against his chest in a bear hug before he glimpsed Libby cornered at the counter.

"Hi there, slim," he greeted her, releasing me but not without slipping me a dirty look. Sure, I was supposed to await him in solitary splendor, my life a vacuum.

"I was just leaving," Libby breathlessly announced lest my violation begin before she managed her escape. She dived into the largest of her shopping bags to extract a slinky feather boa long as an intestine.

"What's the hurry? It's a pleasure to see you." Leo swaggered to the counter to deposit his offering. He pinched Libby's concave cheek. She turned to stone.

"How do you stay so thin?" He pinched his own midsection. Leo likes to squeeze flesh, even his own. A man of appetites.

"I eat sensibly. I keep on the move. I swim twenty laps a day." Libby divulged her fascinating secret, graciously including me in her audience.

"Don't exaggerate it, kid; leave something on your bones for a man to grab hold of," he dictated in his paternal fashion. At the suggestion of such an eventuality, Libby commenced to garrote herself with the snowy plumage, twisting the sinewy muff 'round and 'round her extended neck, a price tag like a religious medal dangling above her sharp collarbone. Leo gallantly reached over to detach the ticket. Libby hit the ceiling.

"Take it easy," he calmed her in his easy New York voice. "At least have a glass of wine for the road."

"Oh, no, thank you, I'm so sorry, I couldn't possibly," Libby hysterically regretted. "I'm late now for my tumbling class. It's my favorite physical fitness course. I've tried to get Hope to go," she bleated, casting a nervous glance in my direction. "Soon we'll have to talk about Africa."

"Africa is an absolutely stunning and amazing continent," Leo supplied.

That sank my heart. I had thrilled to his opinions on numerous topics, but never on a vast continent.

"Did you shoot many animals?" I asked.

"Only with cameras," the humanitarian assured me. He seemed surprised to discover I was still around.

I moved in closer to the fascinating couple. "Wasn't that awfully tame for Mrs. Hermann?"

Leo's face closed like a louver.

Libby shot to the door, but Leo, trained in such hostly matters, got there first, and the team fell into a danse macabre in the tight foyer till Leo got smart and froze in his tracks. Libby flapped around him, avoiding body contact, glancing at me, her buzzard head held high.

"Till tomorrow." She clasped her bags to her chest. "We'll be here at about two or two-thirty."

"Don't hurry lunch on my account."

Libby wheezed gleefully and then, caught in her paroxysm, put her mouth close to Leo's ear. "Tell Hope to behave like a lady," she commissioned him in a stage whisper, and, feathers flying, swooped out.

"If someone doesn't throw a fuck into the broad soon, she's

going to eat herself up alive." Leo pensively shook his big head and came toward me with his familiar rolling gait. Leo was once a merchant seaman. He'd been a lot of manly things—a boxer, a teamster, a dockhand, a Communist, a bartender—before he made his mark as café society's pet host, as well as my cheapskate lover.

"You're the best-looking thing I've seen in a month," he said, squinting at me. "Why is it always so dark in here? What are you running, a speakeasy?" He pulled a silk ribbon hanging from the Japanese lantern floating above the counter, and we were bathed in an orange glow. He made a disgruntled face. Leo finds my lighting depressing, as do I, but trust me, the dungeon would not benefit from the merciless glare of spotlights.

He swung his arms around my stiff shoulders and locked his hands at the nape of my neck. "Hey"—he gave me an affectionate shake—"aren't you glad to see me? Say something."

I said something: "What's in the bag, Leo?"

"That's how you greet your lover after a cruel separation?" he teased me. "God, I missed you. I was ready to jump out of the plane before it landed."

"But you didn't jump, did you?" I said. I just love it when people boast about what they almost did.

Leo laughed. His laugh is a brief and amazed bark, as though amusement comes as a surprise. He bent down and kissed me on the top of my head. I did not melt.

"You're tough," he joked, and finally gave some attention to the neglected parcel he'd delivered to the counter. "Let's see what's in here," he mused half to himself. "Well, there's this." He flourished a bottle of wine. "Good, lovely." He expressed his satisfaction as he studied the label. "I stopped off at Leopold's to make sure the barn hadn't burned down, and Paul was just unpacking a few cases of the new Beaujolais. He tells me it's a vintage year. So I told him to wrap one up for me." Paul was Leo's day manager. So the wine was probably the boss's complimentary bottle. "Let's see what else he threw in." Leo dug deeper into the bag and fished out a flat wax paper package. He winked at me. My heart, as they say, skipped a beat.

He took care of opening the surprise himself, unfolding the waxed wrapping and regarding the contents with pleasure. "How thoughtful of Paul," he said with genuine appreciation. "Genoa salami. The real stuff." Affection crinkled his features. The presentation was over. The bag was empty. He absently smoothed the wrinkled paper, flattening and neatly folding the used paper bag just in case I had some future use for it. I sat there like a stone statue.

Leo nervously rubbed his palms together. I could see how aggravated he was becoming. "Let's try this batch of wine," he cheerfully suggested, employing the hearty skills that made his restaurant such a hit. He reached for a slice of salami and chewed on it as he slipped behind the counter. He found the corkscrew hanging on its customary hook. He found two long-stemmed crystal goblets in the curtained kitchen cabinet. He blew dust off them. He set them on the counter. Then he took up the bottle again. He uncorked it with a muffled and expert pop. He lifted the cork to his nose. He smelled it. He smelled the lip of the bottle. I thought he'd smell his rotten loafers before he judiciously poured an inch of red wine into one of the long-stemmed wineglasses. He sloshed the ruby liquid to the bowl of the glass, smelled the contents for a while, and finally, gravely, took a speculative sip of the potion. My arbiter of good taste!

"Not bad." He filled both glasses and held one out to me. "Here, sweetheart," he said, "tell me what you think of it."

I didn't move a muscle.

He came out from behind the counter and sat on the adjacent stool. He drummed nervously on the milk-glass top, examining me. "Have you eaten anything today?" he asked, as though that might explain my cranky mood. He picked up a slice of salami and held it to my closed lips. "Taste," he coaxed me.

I pushed his hand away. "Stop feeding me! What do you think I am, this collection of orifices that need to be stuffed? This alimentary canal you have to keep filling?"

Leo winced. "Hope," he said softly, "you know I didn't want to make that trip to Africa."

"It seems you never do what you want to do." It hurt my throat to talk.

He took my hand and rubbed it between his warm palms. "Sometimes I do." His voice got thick with lust. "Let's get into bed, Hope." He looped his fingers through mine.

"Bed!" I yelped. "You think you can just walk in here and march me right into bed?"

Leo stroked my hair. I could almost smell the sex hormones, a musk coming off his breath. Despite his ordinary, middle-aged looks, Leo is a tireless, a marathon sexual freak.

"Do you have a better suggestion?" He rubbed my neck.

"Forget about it, Leo. We are not going to bed."

"Hope," he said, "don't give me a hard time."

"I don't intend giving you any kind of time."

I could see how sorry he felt that such a wonderful person should suffer such a shitty reception.

He put his hands in the pockets of his corduroy pants and sat for a long time unhappily regarding me. "How long am I going to be punished for taking a trip I thought was a ridiculous idea in the first place? I had no choice. After all these years of Muriel being stuck in the house, could I say no to her? I missed you like crazy. I couldn't stop dreaming about you," he said in tender accusation.

"What makes you so sure you're not still dreaming? Maybe I'm not real. Maybe I'm nothing but a figment of your imagination. An erotic fantasy. What do you think, Leo, do you think I'm a genie who lives off kerosene inside a lamp when you're not around?"

He laughed his short bark of a laugh. He reached for me and hugged me. He caressed my neck. He acted as if we'd declared a truce. "You're the sexiest fantasy alive." He kissed my ear.

I pulled myself out of his clutches. "I'm not a fantasy, Leo. I'm real. I'm a real flesh-and-blood woman with real everyday needs not solved in your dreams!"

I'd never seen such incomprehension settle on Leo's innocent face.

"I know you're real, Hope. I've never met a realer woman." He squeezed my thigh.

"Maybe that's my problem," I sullenly replied. "Maybe I'm too real. A real fool, here for the taking. Go home," I shouted, unable to endure another moment of his pained expression.

"I didn't expect you to be this angry." Leo made a sad admission. He was aging before my eyes, going all gray and lined, like the mad scientist whose secret serum is wearing off. "I knew it wouldn't be easy today, Hope, but I didn't expect it to be this bad."

"Perhaps your dreams misled you, Leo. Go home," I wailed with exasperation. "You have a home, don't you? That place uptown where you pay the electricity and the telephone and the laundry bills! Go get your money's worth."

A subtle expression of alarm replaced Leo's pain. "Are you asking me to pay your bills? Is that what you're saying?"

"No, I'm asking you to go home."

"You want me to help you out, Hope? Is that it? You need some help?"

"Not if you go willingly, I don't."

"Don't be so defensive. Talk to me. Communicate with me. Be specific. Tell me what you need, and if I can, I'll be only too happy to supply it." His expression turned tragic at the prospect of so much happiness.

"I need to be on a space shuttle to Mars by tomorrow afternoon. Can you supply that?" My eyelids fluttered as if a flock of gnats had flown in. I fought back tears.

Leo was all over me in a flash. "Sweetheart, darling baby," he crooned to me, rocking me in his arms, "what's the matter? Why are you so upset? Don't you know how much you mean to me? I didn't want to leave my sweet baby, not for a minute." He massaged my back, kneaded my shoulders. His hands felt strong and comforting.

"Better?" he said when I surfaced from my crying jag. He had recovered from his age attack, as though my tears had restored his youth.

"Leo, there's been an awful development in my life."

He handed me a glass of wine, his Semitic features so filled with compassion and concern you'd gladly have sold him an exclusive on your forthcoming suicide.

"Let me dry my girl's tears," he said, pulling a crumpled handkerchief from his jacket pocket. As he dabbed at my cheeks, a tiny tissue-wrapped object fell onto my knees.

"What's this?" I asked, plucking it off my lap.

"Oh, Jesus," he groaned, "I almost forgot. It's a little something I brought you from Nairobi."

"For me?" I fluttered my lashes at him. "Leo!"

"It's nothing, really," he modestly insisted, and as it came to pass, truer words have rarely been spoken.

"Oh," I said, "you remembered!" I tore off the fragile tissue paper.

"It's nothing, Hope," he repeated.

I held the nothing in my hand. It resembled a wire loop.

"What is it?" I was compelled to ask.

"It's a bracelet," he explained, endeavoring to force the vile coil over my fist onto my wrist.

"Are you sure?" I held the black loop between my pincer fingers.

"Well, what does it look like?" Leo's face was flushed. "They sell them at the terminals. It's a genuine elephant hair. They're supposed to bring good luck. I got one for Cynthia, too." He exhausted his sales pitch with a bleak smile.

"An elephant hair," I rejoiced, dropping the lewd apparatus to the floor. "How sweet. And how *appropriate!* Any mature woman who gets an animal whisker suitable for a twelve-year-old girl to mark an anniversary certainly needs all the luck she can find!"

"Hope," he groaned, and stooped over to retrieve the treasure, which he wisely returned to his pocket. "I'll buy something nicer for you tomorrow. I promise I will."

"Don't be silly," I said. "Who am I to get something nicer?" His cheap face shimmered before my eyes.

"Damn it!" His palm slapped the counter. "How many times do I have to tell you I'm no good at this gift-giving business? I forget, Hope. In twenty years I've bought Muriel three presents, tops."

"How nice for Muriel." I gulped down a swallow of wine.

"No, no, what I mean is I'm an old married war-horse. It's been a long time since I've done any courting." He grimaced at the quaint term. "When Muriel wants something, she tells me, and that's that."

"I see," I said.

He looked doubtful. "What do you see?"

"I see the same thing you see. You only know how to be married, so go home and be married. Let your wife entertain you."

"I don't consider you entertainment, Hope. You're much more to me."

"That's too bad," I told him. "I can't afford these serious feelings you harbor for me, do you understand? You're having them at my bankrupt expense. Get out of my hovel!" I shouted, at which point we were disturbed by the ring of my off-white telephone, snug at the foot of my chaste bed.

I sidestepped my way across the dark living room, fell on the mattress, and picked up on the third ring. "Hello?" I said.

"Hello, sweetheart," a confidential voice nudged me. "Have you been thinking about me?"

"Compulsively, Rush," I playfully answered. Why thwart the megalomaniac?

"Good girl." He gave me a verbal pat on the behind. "I have to talk fast," he said in his usual pressure-cooked style. "About tonight, I'm stuck at the finals, so I'm going to be late."

"Oh, that's okay, Rush, I'm running late myself."

"Connors is incredible," he barreled along. "Are you watching it on the tube?" And as he spoke, I heard a great swelling of assembly-line human voices supplying the background.

"Watching what?" I asked with the uncanny rapport that has marked our relationship since its inception.

"You're beautiful." He chuckled enigmatically, and there was another appreciative roar from the crowd, just as Leo materialized at the foot of my bed, swinging the wine bottle in one hand, our glasses in the other. He lowered himself to the mattress with an audible exhalation of fatigue.

"Who's that?" Rush demanded in his trigger-happy voice. "Where?"

"Don't let whoever it is damage the goods, doll," Rush said with a final laugh, and click, we were disconnected.

Never, not once since the commencement of our lighthearted fling, has Rush allowed me the last word, up to and including a measly good-bye. But I forgive his immature need to control. As I've vainly tried to explain to my closest friend, Marshall Springer, one can't expect a high-strung individual such as Rush, who had the misfortune to run over his own mother in a bizarre no-fault vehicular fatality, to be your ordinary Mr. Nice Guy.

"Who was that?" Leo propped himself against the pillows.

"It was my broker," I said. "He wants me out of the money market."

Leo scowled. "You made your point, Hope."

"My point was for you to go home, Leo."

"I don't want to go home. I want to stay here with you." He

pulled me against his chest. His pungent male odor filled my nostrils.

I squirmed to free myself. "Leo," I said, "it's over. We're finished."

"No, it's not over." His hand brushed my breast; his thumb outlined my nipple. I shivered at the tingling sensation. I was getting fed up with fighting for my principles.

"Do you know how beautiful you are, Hope?" Leo's eyes were dizzy with desire. "With your beautiful red hair." He stroked my shoulder-length hair and scratched my scalp.

"The color is auburn," I said.

"And your beautiful red mouth." He slipped a finger between my lips, but I kept my teeth tightly clenched.

"And your beautiful red eyes." He traced the shape of my eyes around the sockets.

"They're hazel." I smothered a laugh.

He moved his hand over the curve of my belly and down to my mound of Venus. "And your beautiful red-hot cunt," he said softly.

"Don't get any funny ideas, buster." I pried his fingers off me.

Leo grunted. "Why do I have to go through this minefield every time we're together, Hope? Why can't you just trust me and relax? I only want to give you pleasure. That's the only thing I'm here for. Why do you keep fighting me?"

"I hate pleasure," I said. "I'm a masochist."

Leo chuckled. "You like pleasure all right. You like it more than any woman I've ever met."

"Really?" I said. "Don't all women like pleasure?" I'd been through this routine with Leo before, innumerable times, but like a child being read a bedtime story, I never tired of the predictable repartee.

"Not the way you do, kid. You never get enough. I relish your greed, Hope." He snuggled closer.

I pulled myself off him and knelt on the mattress. "Some greed," I lamented, and a warm wave of melancholia washed over me. "You know who's coming to see me tomorrow? My ex-husband Babi's present wife. You know what my ex-husband does for a living? He owns a country. It's a family concern. They employ about twenty million slaves who are satisfied to work for nothing. So you can imagine the profit the business shows. And this," I said, waving my arms at my poverty, "is what I have to show for all my fabulous greed."

Leo folded his arms behind his head and leaned against the wall. "Babi? Wasn't that the Iranian student you were married to?"

"He's not Iranian; he's Ustanian. They're completely different cultures."

"How interesting," Leo said, stifling a yawn. "You married him so he could get a green card, didn't you?"

"I certainly did not. Babi didn't bother about papers and cards and all that bureaucratic claptrap."

"Didn't you tell me he was up on drug charges—or inciting-to-riot charges—and was in danger of being deported if you two didn't marry?"

"So," I fired back, "is making your mother happy the only valid basis for a meaningful marriage? We were divinely suited. We were an ideal couple."

Leo preferred not to express an opinion. He reached down to the floor for the wine bottle and refilled our glasses.

"It's so humiliating," I moaned, my body jolted by a wave of hot pain. "That calculating majorette from New Jersey is going to visit me here, find me still stuck in this pig trough, everything unchanged except that it's five years later."

"Here, drink something," he suggested in his soothing manner.

"Stop pushing that cheap wine on me!" I slapped his hand

away. "Anyway, why are you still here, poaching on my preserves?"

"We need to talk, seriously. Let's work out an arrangement, Hope, one we can both live with."

"We can't have an arrangement, Leo. Forget it."

"Don't be so stubborn, so eager to end things. You put in a year softening me," he said with a martyred smile. "Why throw it away? We're two intelligent people; we should be able to negotiate something."

"A negotiation!" I exclaimed. "How thrilling. Maybe I should get an attorney to represent my interests."

Leo made a sour face.

"You won't need anyone to represent you. Trust me, I'll be fair. I'm no Rockefeller," he divulged with a heartbreaking smile, "but I think I'm a pretty decent fellow."

"*Fair!*" I recoiled at the insulting term. "What do I care about fair? I didn't love and lose a prince for fair! I hate fair. I piss on fair."

"What *do* you want, Hope?"

"I told you. I want you to go home. The party is over."

"I don't want to go home," he whimpered like a spoiled child.

"Leo," I exploded, "how long could this cushy deal of yours go on? You think I can just write off the next couple of years? That I have a pipeline to the Fountain of Youth?"

He sighed. "For me you do." His fingers reached out to touch my hair. "I guess I haven't been thinking much," he ruefully conceded. "I've been too busy having a good time. If I've been selfish, darling, I'm sorry. I never meant to take advantage of you. It was like being a kid again—coming down here. . . ." His voice trailed off.

"You were experiencing an optical illusion. You are not a kid. I'm not your high school sweetheart. You can't come sneaking down here for a quick *shtup* while my mother is out playing canasta."

"Quick?" He scanned me with sly blue eyes.

"What do you want, a Medal of Honor, Leo?"

He heaved a deep sigh at the injustice of it all and swung his legs around to sit hunched up at the edge of the mattress, his knees higher than his bent head.

I put my hand on his stooped shoulder. "An arrangement wouldn't work, Leo. Believe me. Respect my womanly instincts. You want it for free. You need it for free. You'd feel cheated if it wasn't for free. Trust me. I know what I'm talking about. You're not the only cheapskate I've known in my life."

He spun his head of gray curls around. "I'm not cheap! No one has ever called me cheap," he hissed through his teeth. "I may not have been generous in certain trivial ways, but you always seemed pretty satisfied with what you were getting."

"Thanks a lot for being a terrific lover," I said coldly.

"It's not a mechanical skill," he said with an affronted air, as if he were *my* victim. "It's the way I feel with you. I love giving you pleasure. I really care about you. Such feelings are rare and valuable. Don't just throw them away, Hope."

I didn't wish to pursue the matter further. "Leo, it's really been grand," I told him.

"Just like that? This is how we say good-bye?" The hurt! The cruelty! The disbelief!

"What did you have in mind," I snapped, "a suicide pact?"

Leo gave up the struggle. He pulled himself off the bed, groaning from the exertion. I turned on my side and curled up into the ever-popular fetal position. I felt his eyes boring into my back, then heard the sound of muffled footsteps navigating the impacted room, and the door opening and closing, and finally the iron gate closed with a clang. I rolled over and stared at the tin-pressed ceiling.

3

Alone, I paced my narrow cell like the caged animal I am, with the slight disadvantage that the lioness, whatever her grief, is not tortured with remorse over a disastrous divorce. How did it happen? How did I lose the prince? I was a pawn of history, that's how. I was crushed in the angry fist of time, a casualty of the so-called counterrevolution mounted by a pack of blood-thirsty hippies who were determined to tear down our pig society and replace it with a marathon love-in. Babi was slow to join the revolt, but once initiated, soon became one of its more ferocious leaders. I *had* to leave him. I *had* to get out of our arsenal of a West Side railroad flat. Even Babi approved the move, deeming it a necessity for a guerrilla chief of his importance to have access to multiple hideouts.

All the cycles of my biorhythm chart must have been joined at their lowest phase when I came across Libby's ad in the *Voice*. "Charming furnished garden apartment in West Village," it read, "woman preferred." Bells should have gone off in my head at the word *charming*. Who bothers with charming when they supply real light, real heat, and real space?

As soon as my subversive husband saw the private entrance on Grove Street, down three steps behind a creaky wrought-iron gate, he was sold on the setup, no doubt running clips of himself crawling on his belly under the front stoop while the dopes from the FBI waited to intercept him in the upstairs vestibule. The garage-sale fittings he found even more intriguing since, as is common with zealots reared in the lap of luxury, Babi had fallen jealously in love with squalor.

"It's only for me," I remember reassuring my future landlady as she cast nervous glances in the direction of the hair ball at my side. "He just came along to protect me from imperialism."

Why flog a dead horse, particularly when the carcass in question happens to be oneself? I moved in. Who notices the absence of advertised gardens in the middle of February? Who worries about inhabiting Fu Manchu's torture chamber when she is living in the shadow of the FBI? Libby and the prince subsequently established such a rapport over a stinking rug and discovered so many similarities in their privileged backgrounds that she willingly rented me the room.

But Libby's storage bin of a basement was never intended to be my home, a permanent break from matrimony. It was a strategy, a holding pattern, to get me out of the direct line of fire and give Babi time to come to his senses. We'd only been married six months, and that after almost four years of inseparable devotion. And we didn't legitimize our four-year bond to get Babi papers, as some ignorant meddlers have hinted. We married as a pledge, a commitment to the uncertain future. Some future! In no time flat Babi's daily visitation rights led to an unprecedented intimacy with Libby, of all people, who promptly proceeded to lose my husband to her best friend and former college roommate, Joanne, another impassioned revolutionary, who was so cute, so pert and fiery in her teeny-weeny military fatigues you'd have expected Barnum and Bailey to snatch up the pygmy and stand her on the back of a pony. I ignored the militant affair. Joanne a serious threat to the survival of my marriage? The idea was laughable.

Now, six years later, I lay upon my bed of pain adrift in a current of reminiscence so powerful I could have reached out and touched Babi as he vividly materialized at the foot of my mattress, languidly requesting a divorce.

"A divorce!" I howled, clinging to the edge of my sinking raft. "Why?" After all, it wasn't as if Babi were hampered by the demands of a nagging wife.

He told me he wished to marry Joanne.

"She'll make your life a hell." I fought his destructive decision. She'd give him not a minute's peace. She was too noble, too roused by injustice to be wife material. Did the dauphin marry Joan of Arc? Did Gary Cooper wed Ingrid Bergman? No, these paragons were allowed to become saints and symbols, not domestic chattel.

He then informed me Joanne was pregnant.

"So what? Have the kid," I magnanimously consented. We'd all collectively parent it. Weren't he and Joanne sworn enemies of the fascistic patriarchal family structure? Weren't parents the reactionary enemies? I was wasting my breath. Babi wished to marry Joanne, and the prince's wishes were fate's commands. The day came when the lovebirds flew off to Ustan to await the birth of their royal child, and I, in a hardly conscious state, flew off to Haiti to accept vows of poverty in a language I never understood.

My remembrance of things past was intolerable without a single salvageable butt in the dungeon. It occurred to me I could die of detoxification before a faithful servant shuffled in to prepare the hookah. Unlike the hunger artist on the top floor of this Georgian mansion, I do not thrill to deprivation. I promptly dialed the Tri-Rite Deli on Sheridan Square to call in my order. I had to grease their palms and add a couple of cans of tuna, a large jar of Nescafé, and a six-pack of Budweiser to get them to deliver my cigarettes, and still the snotty clerk wouldn't allow their delivery boy to stop off at the newsstand and get me a copy of today's *Post*. Believe me, it's the petit bourgeois shop owners of this world, not the idealistic Babis, who will succeed in bringing the whole circus crashing around our ears.

I made my next crucial call to my oldest and dearest friend and adviser, Marshall Springer. I listened to the phone ringing in Marshall's congested file cabinet of an apartment on the fifth floor of a St. Mark's Place walk-up. Marshall is another pauper.

He teaches a course on film at Cooper Union, an occupation he detests, and supplements his untenured income by writing articles no one understands on films no one has seen that are published in quarterlies no one reads. He picked up on the fifth ring.

"Hello." He sounded extremely weak.

"Marshall? It's me."

"Hope, thank God I was able to get to the phone. I have a very serious question to ask."

"Shoot," I said.

"Can a person die from eating a green liverwurst sandwich?"

Dr. Diamond got on his case. "A Jewish person can."

"Don't make me laugh," he pleaded. "I'm in too much pain."

"Why did you eat it, you dope? You know liverwurst is against your religion."

The reason I alluded to Marshall's faith was to impress on him that I am not in favor of his joining the only gay congregation in the far-flung Jewish conspiracy. Of all the ideologies I have endured vis-à-vis Marshall Springer, from his being a Communist in high school, along with the other hunchbacks, to a brief flirtation with Catholicism induced by a sexual trauma under the Coney Island boardwalk, to his ardent defense of the Vietcong at the side of my radicalized husband, nothing, no dogma has appealed to me less than his charging out of the closet in a slavish impersonation of his card-carrying Hadassah mother, the Inconsolable Widow, Mrs. Natalie Springer.

"Oh, I don't know," he fretted. "I've been sitting here all afternoon clocking some fabulous buns in white shorts and I got an attack of the blind munchies and figured why not?"

"Are those the tennis finals you're talking about?" I made an educated guess.

"Is this Hope Diamond?" came his startled rejoinder.

True, I'm not reputed to be much of a sports nut, but my

horizons have considerably broadened since the advent of Rush.

"Rush called from some tennis game to say when he'd be over," I negligently dropped. "Marshall, I need some brilliant counseling."

"G-o-l-l-y," Marshall drawled, "we almost talked a whole sixty seconds before you dragged Hitler's name into the conversation."

"Hitler" is Marshall's jealous sobriquet for my latest conquest. It is Marshall's contention that while he cruises Christopher Street in a tireless search for evil storm troopers, only to find pussycats under all the leather and chains, I had but to drop into Leopold's on the night of Leo's departure to waltz out with the real thing.

"Happy child." He was still gloating. "Have the whips and blindfolds come back from the cleaner's yet?"

"Please," I begged him, "could we stay off your fetishes for just a minute? I have such terrible news."

"How terrible?" He haggled with me.

"That shadow just left," I said, referring as we sometimes do to Skinny Libby, "and did she drop a bomb on me!"

"Get yourself the best lawyer in town" came his instant response. Where was he with all his smarts when I divorced the prince and settled for a pittance?

"I'm ready to kill myself, and you're cracking jokes," I bleakly accused him.

"This better be good, Hope," he warned me.

"Joanne is back in town. Libby had lunch with her!" I broke the story.

Marshall received the bulletin in stony silence. "Hold it, babe," he said after a pause. "I need a smoke."

I listened to the sounds of him maneuvering around his file cabinets.

"How did Libby react?" were his first words when he got back on the horn.

"Libby! What does Libby have to do with this? It's *my* husband the bitch confiscated, remember?"

"No," he groaned. "Don't do this to me. I'm probably dying of unkosher botulism. I've smoked one thousand last cigarettes. I've been pinned here like a suicide note to the TV watching two anti-Semites hit a ball back and forth, and you want to start on your bullshit about 'my husband, the prince'!"

I ignored his outburst. "Libby has arranged for me to see Joanne tomorrow. That drone is going to sit here, in this smelly tunnel, weighed down by her ruby and emerald crown, showing me snapshots of the heir apparent. Help!"

"How help?" He inhaled in short, explosive spurts. "By my lights you're well rid of the prince. One, he's a filthy Arab, and two, he was too short for you."

"He's not an Arab. He's Ustanian. Ustanians are crazy about Jews. We're their best customers." I found myself debating international political issues. It's no picnic to be the pawn of global tensions. My condolences to Helen of Troy!

"Get off it, Hope." I heard myself rebuked. "I can remember that little bastard getting all hot over Israel's persecution of the Palestinians. He deserves a dumb *shiksa* like Joanne, who also happens to be the right height for him."

Do people ever look at anything but their wonderful selves? Yes, Marshall is tall. If nothing else, he is tall. After an agonizing adolescence, during which it was an act of mercy to know him, he shot up to six foot three, round shoulders and all. His infatuated mother considers him tall, dark, and handsome. Tall and dark I'll give her, but handsome is definitely in the eyes of the beholder. On that subject, all I will say is that the world is not less alluring since Marshall chose to bury his features in a darkened cinema.

"Will you be serious?" I pleaded.

"Well, I still have about a quarter of a pound of liverwurst left. You're welcome to it."

"I'm coming over right now to eat every morsel of it!"

"Good God!" I could taste the contempt my agitated state had provoked in him. "I can't believe this fuss you are making over a lightweight like Joanne. Are you becoming senile? Why are you flipping over an extra, a bit player?"

"That bit player is living my life," I said with bitterness.

"Ah, how interesting. I wondered who was doing the honors."

"I had an investment in the prince. A future, a marriage." My voice went shrill.

"Oh, boy," Marshall sighed, "I never dreamed when I picked up the phone I was going to have such a good time."

At that worst possible moment, the Tri-Rite order arrived.

"Don't hang up," I yelled into the receiver. "If you're not on the line when I get back, I swear I'm going to wrap this tangled cord around my neck and jump off a mountain of Libby's knickknacks."

The delivery boy turned out to be the pride of the Gray Panthers as he laboriously wended his way to the counter, gazing about him with eyes never too old to be amazed.

"Is this a temple or something, lady?"

"It's a funeral parlor," I barked, and shoved a substantial portion of my monthly stipend into his fist. I ushered him out fast and raced back to the phone, tearing open one of the Vantage packs.

"Are you still there, Marshall?"

"Yeah, but going fast. All my extremities are slowly going numb, especially my tongue. Hope, do you think it would help if I sucked on a lemon?"

"That would be a refreshing change. Marshall, give me one of your brilliant scenarios. Should I leave town? Should I let her in? How the hell am I going to handle this audience with Princess Joanne?"

"Okay, Hope, here goes. The way I see it play is, you get down on your knees and kiss Joanne's feet for taking that murderous *putz* off your hands."

That knocked the wind out of me. "How can you be so vindictive? So hard on Babi? Who did he ever murder? He worshiped you."

"Princess Ida, why are we having this dispute? Did I tell you to leave him? Did I tell you to get nausea attacks every time he attempted to approach your Judaic sheets? Did I make you fall out of love? I'm not a well man. Let me die in peace."

"I never stopped loving him. We had a small crisis, that's all. I still love him."

Who on this vile planet could understand my complex ties to the prince? He had been my lover, my husband, my support, my friend, my father.

I was not prepared for the attack my confession provoked.

"Dummy," Marshall yelled. "I thought I'd be saying prayers for the dead over you by the time you had the sense to split from that junkie!"

"He wasn't a junkie. He just experimented with drugs the way everyone, including you, experimented."

"Not with the hard stuff I didn't. I'm not as brave and fearless as you."

"Why are you being so sarcastic?" I took another slug of Leo's choice wine. It slid down a constricted passage knotted inside my throat. "Can't I express any natural regret about the failure of my marriage?"

"It wasn't a failure!" Marshall railed at me. "It was a triumph. A fabulous success. To behave the way you behaved, to take those risks and walk away from the situation not only alive but with five thousand clams a year? It should only happen to me," he slipped in a side order to his Maker. "And then, at curtain time, when it was apparent to all that the prince had to go home fast if he was going to get there at all, to pull a rabbit, a human sacrifice like Joanne, out of the hat so he went quietly, willingly. It was inspired, a coup. And now you've decided to sing the marriage blues?"

"Some sacrifice. That undersized New Jersey baton twirler is living in a castle on the Caspian with servants fawning all over her."

"In that fucking oil field. How long do you think you'd last there, Hope, without your telephone and your deliveries and your game shows and the talent you lure into your cave?"

"But that's everything I want to change," I eagerly answered. "It's all so pointless. So boring. So humiliating. That's precisely why I just threw Leo out."

"Leo?" My mentor broke in with a delighted exclamation. "Good old Leo. When did he get back?"

"Too soon," I said.

Marshall laughed. For reasons too provincial to mention, he is Leo's number one fan. "How did he look?"

"Cheap," I said. "Extremely cheap."

Marshall whinnied with laughter.

"You know what he brought me from his globe-trotting adventures? An animal hair. A greasy follicle plucked from a dead beast's nostril."

"Hee, hee, hee." Marshall choked on his laughter.

"So you'll understand," I said, "if I ask you never to mention Leo Hermann's name to me again."

"You're a dope," Marshall rejoined.

"I'm a dope," I fumed. "One whole year this guy is hanging around me, violating me, abusing me, and what does he bring me in gratitude? A free sample of wine and, for a special bonus, a few slices of salami. Here, eat some salami, let me molest you, and get out fast."

"Yumm," Marshall said. "Such room service! It should only happen to me that an admirer comes to the door, brings food, gets the juices flowing, and then vanishes like a gentleman. It's not like you wanted to go dining and dancing with the sucker."

"Marshall, are you suggesting I am a sexual pervert such as you who separates my lust from all human and sane considerations? Because I'm not! I'm a normal woman, and the least a mediocrity such as Leo should do is reward me for putting some ecstasy into his mingy life! If not, I'd like to know what I'm doing."

"Don't knock it, Hope," Marshall answered. "You were looking pretty sleek and purring like a cat all year. He must have been doing something right."

How deeply I regretted my accolades to Leo's sexual prowess, but what was I supposed to brag to Marshall about? These armloads of gifts he was showering on me?

"Well, he wasn't exactly doing it with a piece of lox."

"That goes without saying," Marshall drawled at me. "Okay, killer." I could detect the breathing pattern that accompanied his sign-off. "You'd better start limbering up for Hitler."

Just like that.

"Marshall," I yelled, "not so fast. We're not finished with Joanne."

"Yes we are."

"But how should I handle her?"

"As always, with your divine scorn. Enough, Hope. Get up, get bathed, get laid, stop monopolizing the Wailing Wall. Call me tomorrow after you've finished off Joanne. God bless," he said, and I heard the buzz of the disconnection.

4

I was still in the pit-of-pits, wedged between the claw-footed tub and the rattan commode, putting the finishing touches to the radiant mask, when Rush rang the bell. I squinted at the reflection in the smoky medicine chest mirror above the swan sink and applied a final line of kohl along my Etruscan-shaped underlids. I am aware of a breed of woman who brilliantly illumines her hospital-white bathroom in order to magnify her every flaw, but such is not my way. There's a limit to self-scrutiny, and anyway, isn't life essentially a question of lighting? When they spirited Margo through the gates of Shangri-la into the blindingly bright sunlit snow, couldn't anyone, Brooke Shields, have played the withering crone? And this was no withered crone glimmering in the shadowed glass. I finger-fluffed my mop of shoulder-length auburn hair and, in no mood to play peekaboo through the bamboo blinds, went directly to the door to welcome my caller.

"Hello, gorgeous." He nuzzled my neck and then pushed me away to arm's length to get a full-figure shot, appraising me with slate-colored eyes. I felt a shudder of sensation at Rush's touch. How explain the mysteries of the human heart? My response to this man may have been genetic. Perhaps he was the direct descendant of the Cossack clan that periodically raped my female antecedents.

"Anybody die?" He chucked me under the chin. It was one of his many jests directed at my preference in raiment. For evening engagements I say a woman can't go wrong in basic black. Tonight I'd selected a black scooped-neck ribbed body shirt that fastened at the snug crotch. Around my trim waist I'd tied an indigo blue Peruvian wraparound skirt, the flared hem of the handwoven fabric brushing the calves of black Charles Jourdan boots I would never in a million years have been able to afford if Babi had not generously wired extra funds to pay for gum surgery that ultimately proved contraindicated.

"Would you like a drink?" I said, chortling at his witticism. "There's some wine in the house."

"Do you have a beer?" he asked, trailing me to the counter.

Did I have a beer? You don't run an operation like this without stocking up on your steady clientele's preferences.

How sad that I hadn't remembered to refrigerate the six-pack till after my ablutions. I squatted at the waist-high refrigerator and handed him up a Budweiser. He carefully folded a garment bag he was carrying over the wicker-backed stool before accepting the refreshment.

"Have you decided to move in?" I joked as I tottered in my high-heeled boots.

"Is that a genuine invitation?" He leered at me. I steadied myself against his hard chest and let him sneak in a quick feel. Rush is not what you'd call an accomplished lover, but his vigor makes up for the lack of finesse. I like to look at Rush. He's just enough inches taller than I and has a hard, thin, muscled body. He's obliged to work out daily in a gym to minimize some crippling wounds he sustained while covering the Vietnamese debacle for a Midwest gazette. Rush hails from the Ozarks, wherever that is, and climbed to the heights of New York on the strength of his journalistic skills. I was attracted to him from the moment I caught a glimpse of his narrow, high-cheeked, beige-complected features ogling me in the angled mirror above Leo's busy bar. Writers and anchor men and agents and such flocked to Leopold's.

Rush tore off the tab and drank straight from the can, tilting back his head of silky beige hair. He made a face as he swallowed. "Warm as piss," he reported, setting the beer can on the counter. "Hey," he protested, noticing the remains of Leo's salami donation, "who's been eating my porridge?"

Was the boy feeling threatened? Too attached? I laughed with my fabled good humor.

He rolled up one of the curling slices and popped it between his finely sculpted lips. "I'm starving," he told me, looking for a place to wipe his greasy fingers and finally settling for a neatly folded brown paper bag lying on the counter. Rush is very fastidious about his person and a bit of a dandy. He was wearing sleek-fitted designer jeans and a metal gray turtleneck sweater, to bring out the color of his eyes, plus the mandatory cowboy boots that gave him a bit more height and a short leather jacket I'd never had the pleasure of meeting before. The navy nylon garment bag was a newcomer, too.

"Are you planning to change for dinner?" I pointedly asked, gesturing at this luggage.

"Dinner, right, I'm starving. All I had today were a couple of lousy hot dogs. Did you catch the end of the match?"

Rush has this amusing trait of never answering a question till you've forgotten you've asked it.

"I'm afraid not," I said apologetically. "I had an incredibly busy day today."

His eyes narrowed suspiciously. If I were required to give a one-word description of Rush, I'd definitely say "suspicious." His attitude toward mankind is not elevating. It is his belief that every one of us is a scheming deceiver, with the exception of the rest of the morons who really don't count. My ability to comprehend his tortured reasoning was surely part of my fascination. On the first night of our affair, if one may so define our lighthearted romp, we really thrashed out the motives behind the recent fracas in Vietnam. Rush was not your run-of-the-mill dove, nor was he exactly a hawk. He took credit for the entire debacle, which he ascribed to journalistic verve. I told him on our opening night about my former husband and how I was a war widow as surely as if Babi had been terminated by friendly fire. Rush was of the opinion that my activist husband should have been so terminated, and when he finished telling me exactly why, he opened up and disclosed a number of intimate autobiographical facts. With just a little urging I had discovered how eager this tight-lipped man was to have a talkathon with a supportive and understanding woman.

"We'd better get the show on the road," he told me, rocking back on his heels. "Let's see." He consulted a dashboard soldered to his wrist. "It's seven-thirty now. If we get to a restaurant by eight and back here by nine, nine-thirty, that should give me plenty of time to get thoroughly violated"—he winked at me—"and get out to Kennedy to catch the L.A. red-eye."

Kennedy! Why did that name have a familiar ring?

"What red-eye?" I confusedly asked.

"The one, babe, I've got to catch tonight in order to be in Los Angeles first thing tomorrow morning. Why else would I drag my gear over here?" With a flick of his finger he solved the mystery of the garment bag.

"Tonight?" I whimpered. Somehow I thought Rush would be around to help me through the Joanne invasion.

"Don't you ever listen to anything I tell you? All week I've been giving you my itinerary."

"Oh," I said.

"I told you that scumbag Don was going through with his asshole idea to devote the September issue to the West Coast."

The aforementioned scumbag was Rush's managing editor on *U.S. Sports,* a publication that would have been little more than a catalogue of jockstraps if not for Rush's scintillating prose.

"But it's still May, isn't it? What does that have to do with September?"

He bent down and gave me an openmouthed kiss. "Don't clutter your pretty little brain with such details," he advised when the kiss was concluded.

I couldn't help wondering if anyone else in America was having as good a time as I. I stayed limp in his embrace and, as I supported myself against his hard chest, had what is commonly called a revelation. The real reason, other than all the obvious ones, that Rush had entered my life was that he could take me up in his mighty arms and break me out of this jail at the crucial moment. Could Rush's departure and Joanne's arrival be ascribed to mere coincidence? I'd have to be an imbecile to disregard the role miracles have played in my survival.

The question was: Did a hick such as Rush have the capacity to cooperate in a miracle?

"Listen, Hope, darling"—he held me away from him—"I'm no happier than you about this fucking wild-goose chase Don is sending me on. He wants *me*"—Rush fingered himself with a thumb—"to do some bombastic bullshit about the quality of fans in L.A. Quality," his voice went mincing in homage to Don. "They sit in their fucking Coliseum and yell at everything, and the big shot producers clutter up the field, snorting coke out of fire hoses and promising every animal a screen test. It's embarrassing, man." He seemed in his distress to overlook my gender as well as my ethnicity. "I need Andy Williams bringing tears of patriotism to my eyes with his stirring rendition of 'The Star-Spangled Banner'? Come on." He jerked my arm. "Let's get out of here and get something to eat."

I speedily assembled my shawl and shoulder-strap bag and went straight for the door to demonstrate how little trouble I'd be as his constant consolation in California.

"You know something, Rush," I girlishly chatted while locking his traveling bag inside headquarters, "with all the places I've visited—Paris, London, Montreal, Miami—I have never, ever been to L.A."

"You're lucky," he said, hustling me up the three shallow steps.

"Lucky to have such a delightful adventure before me?" I put a playful twist on his pronouncement.

He grunted. "Do you know what it's like to spend time in that desert of smog? It's like having your sinuses cauterized." He latched the gate behind us.

"You and Lawrence of Arabia," I said slyly, and then, without dropping a beat, I inhaled the foul air with an exclamation of pure pleasure. "Look at the stars," I urged him, till I took a closer look at the leaden sky and realized there were none. "Well," I amended, "the place to look at the stars is in the desert. I hear the skies in the desert are the most thrilling panorama an earthling can behold."

Rush pretended not to hear or perhaps had truly missed my flight of poesy. He walks fast, a squire traversing his fields, so we began our wired sprint east.

"Where are we going?" I ventured to ask.

"To Alfredo's," he said with no hesitation. Rush is not one of your spiritual misfits who stand around on one leg, wondering if he craves Chinese or French or Greek or Japanese or Mexican. No. Alfredo's had yet to poison him, so why look for trouble?

"My favorite restaurant," I said with my legendary cheerfulness.

For some inscrutable reason his level stare hardened.

I forced my hand into the crook of his black leather sleeve and hopped and skipped to keep pace with his athletic stride. Rush's cowboy heels tapped out a victory message to all the miserable and mindless yokels he had so ambitiously left behind. He loves New York with an uncritical and absolute love. Nothing, not the madness and crime rampant on the pitted and perilous pavement, or the breakdown of every conceivable service, or the filth, the black hedges of overflowing garbage bags lining the curb, nothing diminishes the satisfaction of his triumphant migration. We waited at the crossing of Seventh Avenue and Bleecker as a nonstop flow of trucks and cars and buses and cabs went hurtling down toward the Holland Tunnel, as if the siren had sounded and the emergency evacuation had begun. How I longed to join the exodus. Rush stood at the corner in a fury, as if the wait were a personal insult.

"Rush, you remember that Ustanian prince I was married to?" Somewhere in my mind that was a lead-in to the big question, the California question.

"You mean that foreign punk?" he answered with a chilly smile.

I brushed the soft hair off his marble brow and said no more.

"Well?" he urged me.

"Let's go, the light has changed." I made a gay dash into the traffic. It was dumb of me to broach the subject before we were inside the candlelit, cozy confines of his favorite trattoria.

We were at the curtained door of Alfredo's, pushing our way in, and I could already hear the congenial hum of the contented patrons when my escort noticed a disturbance up ahead.

"What's that?" he asked, pulling me out of the entranceway of Alfredo's.

"What?" I asked, pushing us forward into the restaurant.

"That, all those lights and all those people. Look, right at the corner of Sixth. Are you blind?"

"Oh, that. It's nothing." I tried again to lead him inside. I had the door open. I could hear the festive tinkling of wineglasses, smell the delightful aroma of spices and herbs.

"Nothing!" He took a step backwards onto the sidewalk to get a better view. "There must be a thousand people there. And look at the lights." He pointed out a high canopy of twinkling lights, his face getting as eager and elated as a small boy's. "And isn't that a Ferris wheel they've got up on the corner? Oh, great, it's a street fair."

"Isn't that nice?" I said. "We must walk through it right after dinner."

Rush was tugging me by the arm, dragging me toward the frightening hordes. I wanted to catapult myself through Alfredo's plate glass window.

"I love those things." He was spinning his head in boyish glee, practically jumping up and down.

"But what about dinner?"

"We'll pick up something at one of the stands. One of those delicious sausage sandwiches. They're the greatest."

"They're poison," I protested as I was helplessly dragged to my miserable fate.

"Boy, oh, boy," he said, his head still spinning, "they don't have fairs like this in Missouri."

"That's because the Mafia doesn't run Missouri."

His fingers were digging into my upper arm. "We'll see the action, and we'll save some time, too." He winked at me. Time wasn't the only thing the big spender would save.

Thus I was led like a sheep into the midst of the impacted flock. The streets were sealed off by wooden horses, and there was a curb-to-curb slow-moving procession pressed into a narrow path between the facing stalls and concessions. How I dreaded and feared humanity en masse. They were bad enough individually, but in packs! I shuddered. Stereos blasted. Rifles fired. Hawkers hollered. A mob scene, dense and mindless as the riots mounted by my darling Babi. Babi. Would I ever see him again? What if I sank to the littered, grease-slicked asphalt to be trampled to death under the hooves of this blind stampede of tourists eating themselves into oblivion? A cold sweat made my body shirt stick to my skin.

Before I knew what hit me, Rush had shoved us to a stand and slapped a hunk of dripping sausage and onion stew into my passive palm. "It's delicious," he chewed at me, taking great, lip-smacking bites out of the monstrosity in his own hand. We trudged along with the rest of the mob.

"Hey, hey." It was Rush's voice. "Wake up." He shook me by the shoulders. "Where the hell have you been drifting to? Not dreaming of my replacement already, are you?"

I smiled and giggled. Women are fodder!

"What do you say?" He waited for an answer.

"To what?"

"To this game, dundercup." He gave me a mock punch on the jaw, inserted a finger into my late mother's gold hoop earring, and tugged at it. A flow warm as blood ran through my heart and into my groin.

I was standing before a roped-off section of the street, filled with demitasse saucers mounted on tin cans.

"This is a game?" I stupidly asked.

"What else does it look like?" He didn't wait for an answer. "The trick," he filled me in, "is to get a coin to stick to the bottom of a plate."

"I see," I said, not trying to conceal my enthusiasm.

A madonna in a print housedress not unlike one of Libby's recent acquisitions sat cross-ankled on a folding bridge chair. Rush waved a five-dollar bill at her, and her indifference turned into infatuation.

"Hey, watch." Rush was already tossing dimes. "Watch me!" He was always crying "watch me." In bed it was always "watch me, watch me." Never a private moment. He was a real challenge after Leo's benign reign. "Come on." He tried to unload some coins on me. "Give it a try. It's fun."

When, dear God, will I use up my quota of fun!

"I'd rather just watch," I replied, to remind him that was enough thrill for me. I moved to the side, caught in his loathsome recreation. He threw dime after dime into the field of saucers, and I listened to them clink against the crockery before dropping between the cans.

"This is tough. She must have greased her fucking dimes," Rush complained, his face a study in intensity.

The festival was one big steaming, smelly vat of grease layering the heavy sky. No stars were visible through the overhead ribs of twinkling lights.

"Rush, please, let's go back to my place. We were going to save time, remember?" I stroked his leather pitching arm. The minutes, the hours when we could have been planning our jaunt were ticking away. I'd need time to throw a few necessities into a suitcase. Did I have a suitcase?

"I just want to land one; then we'll go," he entreated me like a small boy.

"You don't need to impress me, Rush." I batted my eyelashes at him.

"I want to win you a prize. Hey!" He stopped dead in his tracks as one of the wretched coins skimmed lazily along the rim of a saucer before dropping into the Vatican coffers. "Shit," my date muttered under his breath.

"What do you win in this stupid game?"

"Canaries." He aimed his chin at a leaning tower of cardboard boxes I had somehow overlooked. I could hear them now, twittering miserably in their shoeboxes.

"It's repulsive. It's sordid. I don't want a canary."

Rush tilted his head back and directed his laugh at the heavy, starless sky. He grabbed hold of me and hugged me. "You'll win me, darling." Had anyone in that multitude of misfits ever encountered a more adorable couple?

"I'm going home," I announced, and stormed off into a wall of people. I didn't let that hinder me. I waded through an opening between two competing calzone stands and reached the sidewalk. I kept walking. Rush caught up with me at the corner of Carmine Street.

"Hey, hold it." He came abreast of me and hung his arm like a heavy yoke around my neck. "You're too high-strung, darling," he crooned into my ear, flicking his tongue inside it. "You mustn't go to pieces when I take you out of your lair." He gallantly cupped my elbow to guide me through the mounds of rubbish.

I understood then why legions of martyrs have gone tight-lipped to their doom. They couldn't pry their wooden mouths open.

Rush made two quick forays into the crowd, first to buy himself a bag of nougats as sustenance for his cross-country flight and then to buy a properly chilled can of beer. He kept looking back longingly at the archway of colored lights.

"They don't have street fairs in L.A. They don't have streets! That's why they don't have real fans. Fans come off the streets, not out of some fucking swimming pool or movie lot." The farther we retreated from the festival, the more disgruntled he became, taking quick gulps of beer. In this congenial frame of mind we retraced our steps to Grove Street.

It was close to ten o'clock when I let us into the peace and quiet of my subterranean shelter. Rush went straight for the cushion couch and divested himself of his leather jacket. He pulled off his boots and stretched out with a loud yawn.

"What a day. I'm bushed. Get your liberated ass out of the kitchen."

"I thought the beer would be colder now."

"I don't want any more. I'm already bloated," the charmer disclosed. "Just get over here."

I went to him. I perched on the edge of one of the stiff cushions.

"Lie down." He made space for me.

"There's something I'd like to talk to you about first."

"Talk! We don't have all night." Rush is not big on precoital chitchat. He dug his thumbs into my shoulders. "You're tense."

"Well, I have this problem, Rush. I mean, a problem that doesn't have to be a problem. It could actually be an opportunity, a wild spree—you know?"

He grunted as he slipped his fingers inside the front of my snug body shirt, inching his way toward my nipple as if he'd dropped it down a grate. "What the hell are you wearing? Are you soldered into armor?"

"It's a body shirt." I twisted around to make his job harder. "They're the best things in the world for traveling."

He pulled my wraparound skirt open and ran his hand over my smoothly encased belly. Between the cuff of the boots and the black underpants my naked thighs gleamed. He got rougher in his search for the opening. "Are you sewn into this contraption?" Then he solved the puzzle and ripped open the metal snaps with one tearing gesture. He stroked my warm white belly and pressed his palm against my flattened bush.

"Ah," he said, pulling me against his chest. "How the hell am I going to survive in that fucking Disneyland without you?"

"That's just it." I tried to sit up. "That's what I've been trying to tell you . . ."

"I hear you, doll," he said as he slipped a few fingers into me. "You're wet. You're always wet. You're always ready."

"With you I am," I whispered into his warm ear. "Rush, take me with you."

"Not this time," he said as he unbuckled his belt and squirmed out of his jeans.

"Yes, this time," I said like a child.

"I wish I could." It was not so easy for him to get the thick words out. "It's impossible." He climbed on top of me.

"Why?" I squirmed to get out from under him.

He stopped mauling me and fell flat on top of me, his face buried in my neck. "Celeste is meeting me in L.A." His heartbeats struck against me like blows.

"Let me get undressed. Let's get into my bed," I said, tasting mouthfuls of his soft hair.

"No time," he mumbled, "no time." And he reached under me and pulled my legs around his hips and entered me with such force I was flattened against the rack of bulky cushions. "You're such good pussy, hot Jewish pussy," he chanted in rhythm to his deep thrusts.

My mind went to a place where words can't follow. I heard myself moan.

"Shh," Rush hushed me. "Shhhh, don't move." He supported himself on palms holding down my shoulders. "Watch me," he cried, "watch me." His pale eyes fastened to mine, and even as I watched, I saw his features disintegrate into an infant tantrum.

"Wow," Rush gasped. "Wow." His heart was beating

against my rib cage. He was still moving around inside me, producing trembly, tiny spasms. "Did you come?" he whispered.

"I came," I said, almost convinced.

"Come some more." He kept on pumping.

"It's enough. Enough." My insides were vibrating. My body recoiled from the exquisite stimulation.

He rolled off me. "Are you sure?" He snuggled into my side. He smoothed my hair. He modestly closed my skirts. He straightened my stiff legs. An embalmer couldn't have been more reverent.

"I'm sure."

"I want you to be satisfied. I'm sorry about Celeste," he continued in a whispery voice. "The asylum is giving her her first outpatient privileges. I have to help her, Hope." He waited a decent interim for my response, and when he got none, he quietly added, "You knew I had a wife, Hope. I leveled with you the first night. I never tried to hide it from you."

I turned my face away.

He checked his watch. I could hear the buzz of the battery. "I'd better hit it," he said, and kissed my cheek before climbing over my prone body.

My body wouldn't calm down. It was beating, pulsating with a nasty energy all its own. Headless chicken time. While he was in the bathroom, I lay without moving, listening to the erratic pulses beating in my body.

He came back, washed and refreshed as if he'd gone for a quick dip in the ocean. He slipped into his clothes and pulled on his cowboy boots. He shrugged into his new leather jacket and then patted all his parts and pockets, appearing satisfied with his inventory.

"I'll call you when I get back." He bent over me, took my hand, and kissed it, and then, like the proverbial thief, was gone.

I wanted to get up and lock up behind him and wash myself, but the strange throbbing immobilized me. It was not a pleasurable restraint. Sirens revved up in my head. Bats in the belfry, thousands of them, beeping and bleeping. Were they warning me that my body was beating itself to death? My secret flesh opened and closed like an underwater plant, or was it an animal? What hole in the universe had I fallen through? I wanted to get into my bed, out of my clothes, behind the safety of the geisha screen. But I was too afraid to risk the move. Could my heart take the additional strain? I took long breaths and counted the spaces between the inhalations and the exhalations. That helped. The trembling was subsiding. I felt Rush's juices seeping down my thigh. I closed my eyes and found my safety in the blackness. My body grew quiet. I couldn't lift my eyelids. I left them closed and called it a day.

5

I woke up having my least favorite dream, if it is a dream—the one in which my frantically alert mind finds itself buried in a dead body, limbs and trunk as paralyzed as a quadriplegic's. My mind tensed and pushed against the black space in a colossal isometric effort. I thought I'd die from the exertion. I found myself panting on the cushion couch, the cords of my wraparound skirt holding me in contorted bondage, my body shirt a tourniquet. My legs were numb, bloodless inside the tight Charles Jourdan boots. I lay there, disoriented not to be in my usual nook behind the geisha screen. Recollections of the previous night and the prospects of today began to flood my system, and with that I knew only too well I was awake. I turned and twisted to free myself from my binding garments. Believe me, Houdini got rich escaping from lesser restraints. The pink-shaded wall sconces on either side of the inoperative fireplace cast their eternal light on the mantel clock. It was twelve o'clock. I had two whole hours in which to revamp my entire life.

I limped on bare soles to the front foyer and set the filled kettle on corroded burners Typhoid Mary would scorn, waiting like an Ethiopian at a water hole for the damned thing to come to a boil. Princess Joanne would no doubt expect to be served a high tea, pots of simmering Lapsang souchong and platters of honeyed sweetmeats, but Her Royal Highness would just have to settle for coffee and Oreos like the rest of us peons unless, of course, she came accompanied by her personal cook, who, as far as I was concerned, could have the run of the house and squat on the Armstrong linoleum to grind her mistress's farina.

I carried my morning mug of coffee into the pit-of-pits. The need to soak in a hot tub was crucial. I turned the heavy faucets on full force and squirted Vitabath under the jet. I crouched at the bottom of the deep, claw-footed tub, spreading my thighs wide to release love's secretions to a hot and watery grave. Out, out, damned spot! I rested my head on the mildewed rubber pillow, aching for a few moments of sweet respite, only to be assaulted by thoughts of Rush. He'd probably landed in California while I'd slept my crippling sleep. The fascist! A flash of mortifying pain jolted my head off the pillow. Why didn't he take me with him? Why was I always left behind? Why were some women embedded with precious stones and carted across continents while their infinitely more attractive sisters were left to rot in sleazy basements? How strange for both Rush and Leo to find themselves married to Madwomen of Chaillot, neither of whom they'd ever dream of leaving behind. Was that my problem? Was I too healthy? Too sane? Was it possible I attracted men who ultimately felt deprived of their customary guilt, a paradox to say the least, because if it was guilt the swine craved, what else but persecution did they imagine our entire scuzzy affairs were predicated on?

When Venus ascended, there were no eager attendants waiting to wrap her in thick Turkish towels, but the healing waters and the mug of coffee had done the job, and my reflection in the fogged-up mirror was surprisingly undamaged, considering Mr. Bigfoot himself had trampled across it. I helped my recovery along by applying a fresh layer of kohl to my eye sockets and slipped into my caftan.

I returned to the stove to fix myself a second helping of caffeine, and listening to the sizzling and spitting of the old copper kettle, I became aware of a similar noise directly outside my barred windows. I raised one of the shades to investigate the disturbance and discovered it was raining hard out there. A spring shower. My spirits lifted. What princess would run around making social calls in such nasty weather? Just as I had convinced myself of this merciful reprieve, I spotted a small and lonely form huddled in my doorway, not only servantless but Libbyless as well. What can the condemned do when the executioner arrives two hours ahead of schedule? Call the police? I opened up to bid Joanne welcome.

"Hello, stranger," I called. "What are you doing outside in this storm?"

"I didn't want to disturb you. I know I'm early." Her face was wet and scared inside a drenched babushka. She lifted herself up on her toes to place a shy kiss in the vicinity of my jawbone.

"Where's Libby?" I asked, searching between the raindrops for my landlady, who may be skinny, but not that skinny.

"I don't know! She isn't with you, is she?" Joanne's troubled features were grouped into an imminent deluge of tears.

"Come in, get out of this wet mess." I patted her as I disentangled myself from her clammy embrace and ushered her into my shabby but dry quarters. "Didn't you two have a lunch date?"

"Yes, we did. She stood me up. I waited and waited for over an hour at the Russian Tea Room. It was so crowded and noisy I couldn't take it any more. I thought I'd better come down here." She posed there, dripping puddles onto the linoleum, as I reeled to the familiar strains of her deep and melodious vibrato.

"Take it easy. Calm down." I helped her out of her transparent slicker, avoiding direct eye contact. Joanne looked terrible, as if she'd shrunk and faded in the rain.

"But what could have happened to her? She's the one who insisted on lunch. Could she have been in an accident?"

"Don't be silly. It's much more likely she's been in Nirvana. She meditates now instead of eating." In my heart of hearts I couldn't help wondering if my treacherous landlady had purposely arranged this enchanting tête-à-tête for me.

"Ha, ha," Joanne laughed, a lilting note of dementia praecox in the refrain. "Still the same funny, sardonic Hope. And you look great. So glamorous! So young!" She gave me a gingerly hug. "And I was so worried about you. I heard all about your emergency dental surgery. Poor thing. How are your teeth now?"

"Splendid, considering how I clench and grind them trying to survive on my income."

Joanne appeared unsure if she should laugh or cry at that one. "Ah, yes, of course." She murmured polite condolences and then invoked her characteristic optimism. "However you survive, whatever it takes, it suits you, Hope. You look fantastic. What a relief after seeing the change in Libby."

She should talk about Libby. The more I saw of Joanne, the greater my confusion and consternation grew. She was swimming inside the folds of a self-belted sleazy green cotton shirtwaist, to which I had naïvely assumed Chock Full o' Nuts held exclusive rights, and on her feet were a pair of wet thick-soled sandals fashioned out of surplus tires. Listen, I understand the low profile protectively adopted by the rich when they venture on a slumming expedition to the lower depths, but nothing could quite justify her humble aspect. The hair the babushka had hidden was a chin-length hank of strings, and her enlarged and nervous brown eyes took up half her pale, pinched face. Never till that moment did I realize how pretty Joanne used to be, with a shiny pelt of glossy brown hair, shiny brown eyes, a short, straight nose, and a mouthful of straight white teeth the Almighty has rarely granted to one of his Chosen People. The next time my nitwit landlady remarks someone doesn't look well, I'll make it a point to have Dr. DeBakey in attendance.

"Don't look at me." Joanne made scrubbing gestures as if to erase the image. "Let me look at you." Her mouth widened to reveal beautiful gleaming white teeth. It was only the dental evidence that enabled me to make a positive identification.

"Sit down," I said when I'd collected my faculties. "Go into the living room." I pointed out the route. "Lie down, if you prefer. We'll wait for Libby in there."

"Oh, yes, thank you, I'd love to see the old place," Joanne intoned at me, and vibrating like a hummingbird, she shot through the archway into the splendors beyond. I followed behind and sank myself into the site of last night's molestations to be out of the path of the bird's frantic flight. She spun around, clasping her hands in front of her narrow bosom, and came to an abrupt halt on the hearth of the inoperative fireplace. After a dramatic pause, the miniature diva lifted her arms as if in supplication to Allah—which would be no sacrilege as the princess had converted to Islam to legitimize the claims of her unborn child—and broke into a throaty incantation.

"I can't believe I'm actually back in this room, with Hope Diamond, and everything is just the way I remembered it. Nothing has changed; it's all still here, those sagging armchairs and that broken-down couch, and the hassocks, and the geisha screen." She pointed out that relic as if she were a guide leading a group through the hallowed ruins.

"Nothing has changed, Joanne, I can assure you of that. Will you please sit down?"

But the tour wasn't over. She flew in a zigzag path to the black marble coffee table and began reverently to pick up and finger every beloved memento on its surface. "Look." She held the bronze monkey in her hand, as if the object were news to me. "And there's the incense burner." She swooped down on that relic.

"Don't leave out the peeling wallpaper and the falling ceiling," I added to her inventory. For a certified princess, all of Libby's garish loot may have been a sentimental delight, but for a perpetual pauper such as myself, they were a Rosetta stone, a record of opportunities lost, passions squandered.

She darted my way and hovered over me. "Joanne, sit," I ordered, and before the words were out of my mouth, she'd lighted practically in my lap, sidling up to me with a suffocating avidity. She was an even more disturbing spectacle in close-up. Was she sick? Was she dying? Was she here to make peace with those she'd injured?

She moved in on me and caught my hands in a surprisingly strong grip. "You're not still angry at me, are you?"

"Angry?" I bleated, trying to pull out of her clutches. "Me angry? Whatever gave you the idea I was angry at you?"

"Well, you never write to me, and you never even mention me when you write to Bahram."

Bahram was Babi's correct name, the one invoked in prayer by hordes of serfs.

"Well, Babi and I, we have a kind of business correspondence," I weakly defended myself.

"Oh, I know, I know, I know how close you two are. But I know you felt we betrayed our principles when we married."

"Oh, God, Joanne." I pulled farther back. "That was so long ago I can't even remember it."

"Good," she said, "good, I'm so glad. I need you to be my friend, Hope."

What was this big friend business? I was never her friend. Libby was her friend.

"Where is Libby?" I fretted, as though her absence were the only flaw in a perfect world.

"I'm glad Libby isn't here," Joanne confessed with girlish complicity. "I'm glad of the opportunity to talk to you alone."

"How nice," I said. "What a lucky coincidence that she isn't here." I wrenched my captured hand free. "Why don't I make us a nice pot of tea, Joanne? Would you like that?"

"I'd like that," she consented. "Dear Hope, you've always been so kind and considerate." Her head dropped to the back bolster, and at last she shut her mouth and then her eyes.

I seized the opportunity to study the still life, baffled by the sickly picture. I admit, I hadn't exactly relished the prospect of Princess Joanne being wafted into my cellar on the Peacock Throne, but I took no pleasure in receiving this wraith, who could have been carted in on a stretcher. Even under the benign glow of my pink lampshades, her complexion remained pale and glassy. The skin beneath her thick, short lashes had a bluish tinge. Her closed lips were chalky. Of course, Joanne was never one to subscribe to the artifices of makeup. Not for prudish reasons, oh, no—she was a sexual rebel, too. But once upon a time, when she was wholesome and dewy-eyed, the fresh-scrubbed look enhanced her appeal; now the natural look was a cruel penance.

I left her to her catnap and tiptoed to the kitchen to slip noiselessly behind the counter. My brain was going a mile a minute. Could she have picked up a wasting bug or parasite in her enchanted kingdom? Then why didn't she simply so announce and not pretend she was a normal-looking person? And why wasn't her husband at her invalid side? There was another possibility; an elusive spark flared and then was gone. I refilled the kettle, pondering the conundrum. The elusive spark returned with more force, more fire. Was it possible this least likely of candidates had discovered the joys of narcotics? It took no special inclination to make that discovery while sharing Babi's royal couch. Even I had enjoyed that stuporous communion for almost an entire harmonious year. But Joanne? She'd always hated Babi's penchant for altering the workings of his consciousness. Then again, she wouldn't be the first wife by a long shot to discover it wasn't the man she had married, but his vice.

I turned from my chores at the stove, and being as I am magnetic if nothing else, there at the counter, her elbows planted on the milk-glass top, sat Joanne, earnestly observing me.

"What kind of tea are you making?" she asked in the guise of conducting a normal conversation.

"Tea, the kind that grows in bags," I snapped, slamming down next to her the teapot that went with the terra-cotta bowls.

She smiled at me. I smiled back. Drugs would solve the mystery. They would explain the pallor, the loss of flesh, the ceaseless nervous exhaustion she manifested. Was she in the throes of withdrawal as she sat there on the high stool, displaying herself in all her pitiable condition? She picked up the gorgeous teapot and, with a small, irrepressible mew of nostalgia, proceeded to caress Libby's crummy crockery. It was more than mortal could bear. The exhibitionist. No way would Joanne have a habit without its being of historic proportions. I rinsed out the terra-cotta bowls and slid them across the counter. She fell in love with those, too.

"Herb teas are so much better for your health." The wreck proceeded to instruct me. "In the East they've been studied for centuries and used to cure all kinds of serious ailments."

It never fails, does it? These junkies who will shove any toxic matter into their ravaged systems invariably draw the line at a refreshing cup of Lipton's.

"Spare me," I implored. "If I get an ailment, I'll take an Alka-Seltzer like a good American. What do you have against tea? I thought you grew the stuff on your Caspian estate."

I intended my good-natured admonition to cheer the wretched creature. *Estate!* There's a word any mature woman could ream a contented tongue around.

"Yes," she confirmed. "We did try to raise tea, but it didn't work out." A tear ran down her cheek and dropped into a terra-cotta bowl.

My fabled composure snapped. "What is going on?" I confronted her. "Tell me, Joanne. Level with me. Are you here for a cure? Are you here to kick a habit? It's no shame. And I'll have to know sooner or later."

"A cure?" She reacted as though the word didn't exist in her vocabulary. "A cure," she said sharply. "You think I'm on drugs?" She pressed her palm against her heart. "Me? On drugs? Do I look that bad?" she asked with ghoulish vanity.

"Well, a vision out of the Perfumed Garden you are not. What's the story, Joanne? Don't tell me you're here to catch up on old friends and the theater."

"No, I'm not," she slowly, painfully confessed.

"And how come you're not with Babi?" I blurted out. "Doesn't the man have eyes in his head? How can he allow you to traipse around the world in your condition?"

"Oh, Hope." She sucked in her lower lip. She shivered, as if she'd heard footsteps across her grave, and sat before me in an obvious state of panic. I got gripped by panic, too.

"Is it Babi?" I leveled at her in a low voice. "Has something happened to Babi? Is that why you're here?"

"Yes," she cried. "Yes, something terrible has happened to him."

My hair follicles went erect. I froze with horror. She scampered off the stool and ran into the living room, streaming a long animal wail of pain. How I got from where I stood to catch her on the cushion couch I do not know. "What!" I shook her. "What's happened to him?"

"He's become cruel and sadistic and a monster and I've left him and I'm never going back, never, never." The words came sobbing out of her as she collapsed across my lap. I fell back against the bolsters in an agony of relief. "Hope, I didn't know what to do, where to go. I had to escape from him, and I left my son, my Abbas."

"It's okay. Shhhh. Easy, easy." I absently stroked her quivering back and tucked some loose strands of her protein-starved hair behind one of her small ears.

"I'm sorry, excuse me." She teethed into the absorbent fabric of my caftan.

"Excuse what?" I lifted her gently off my knees. "I never said when you entrapped my husband you had to be happy with him."

"Happy?" She lifted a startled face to me, and all I can say is forgiveness performs miracles because there was a marked improvement in Joanne's flushed and moistened demeanor. "I never knew I could be so unhappy. I never knew there was anyone so cruel." She stared blankly into space.

I held up a restraining hand to stem her emotional flow. "Joanne," I said, "I am sorry to see you in such a state, truly I am, and I have no doubt of your misery, but please, do not make me your confidante. I am totally loyal to Babi. I cannot be an impartial witness. Please don't discuss your marital woes with me. Discuss them with Libby—she's your friend. Discuss them with your mother. Are you and your mother back on speaking terms?" The New Jersey–born and –bred princess had long ago had a serious break with her mother, a registered nurse, due to the woman's craven identification with her oppressors.

"Yes, we've made up, but I don't want to tell her this news yet. I haven't told Libby either," she guiltily admitted. "I was too ashamed. And she seemed so happy for me I couldn't get the words out. Oh, Hope"—she buried her face in her hands— "I had to leave my darling Abbas behind with that monster."

I stopped her again. "Don't, Joanne. Stop. I'm not the right person for you to confide in. I don't even recognize who you're talking about when you call Babi heartless and cruel and a monster. It's not the Babi I know. To me he's always been and always will be a gentle and generous prince."

She sent me a conspiratorial sidelong glance. "You know him better than that. No one knew Bahram better than you. Look at me." She stuck her face in mine. "Take a good look. Do I look like the wife of a gentle and generous prince?"

I hated her insistence on unburdening herself to me. "Yes," I shouted, "yes. That's exactly how you look. I know how you flourish on strife and injustice. Yes, I think you look like death because my Babi has been killing you with kindness."

She sat blinking at me, mad pulses dancing around her eye sockets, and then broke into a cackling laugh. Her laughter was as merry as the Inquisition.

"Please," I requested for the hundredth time, "don't freak out, Joanne. You're tired. You've just been on a flight that would exhaust a perfectly contented person. You know what you should do?" I rhetorically asked, and then promptly supplied the response. "*Nothing.* Simmer down. Relax. Get hold of yourself. Don't say things you'll later regret."

"I have to talk, Hope. I have to let it out. I've been so miserable, so alone. He's shut me out completely!" She captured my unguarded hand. I could have screamed. "For years I've wanted to come to you, apologize to you, beg your pardon for ever suspecting you were jealous of me. You were trying to help me, you were trying to warn me, weren't you? I was so ignorant, so undeveloped then. Despite all the rhetoric in my heart, I didn't trust women. He hates women," she continued in a fierce and resonating whisper. "He's so afraid to appear weak or needy or human. I could pity the man if he wasn't destroying me. He has no heart, Hope. He's dead. He's empty." Her eyes pleaded for my consent.

"You see," I protested, "you're doing it again. My Babi does not hate women. Of that I am sure, because I was there when he discovered us! He was so overwhelmed I thought the discovery would kill him. What is it, can't you have a rupture in your marriage, like everyone else in the world, without turning yourself into some kind of cause? I've had a few problems, a few disappointments with men, too. I'm aware of the fact that they're not perfect."

"You've never known what it's like to belong to a man, Hope, to be his property, his possession. You can't imagine . . ." She fell into a stupefied silence.

"Why don't you go into the bathroom, Joanne? Wash your face. Press a cold cloth on your eyes. It'll take the puffiness right down, and I guarantee you'll feel a lot better."

I could have been talking to the wall. "We shouldn't have gone to Ustan," she meditated aloud. "Ustan has destroyed whatever chance he had to learn to feel. He has no feelings, no real feelings. He doesn't care about anything, except making his palace more magnificent and sitting up there pretending he's a god. And gods don't question themselves. Gods don't explain their actions. They only express their displeasure." She pressed her lips tightly together, pulled her knees to her chest, and gently rocked herself back and forth on the cushion couch. Her intensity was alarming. It took up all the space, it used all the oxygen in the cramped room. My poor Babi. He'd had five years of this harridan's parading herself around like a wreck so everyone could immediately perceive how deprived she was. That was some goddess Mr. God had got stuck with. She came out of the huddle. "He won't even acknowledge how much he hates me. How can you hate what you don't see or hear or notice? I wonder," she said with a small cough of a laugh, "if he'll even notice that I've left him. He might, if someone has the audacity to ask him where I am. I wonder what lie he'll make up. He'll never admit his wife ran away without his almighty permission."

She had lost me completely.

Again the eerie cackle. "Do you know," she said, "it doesn't feel real that I was ever there? I can't even picture Bahram in my mind. Only Abbas is real." Her face began to crumble at the mention of her son's name.

"If you're so sure you're never going back, why didn't you bring Abbas with you?" I innocently asked.

She looked at me as if I were the crazy one. "He'd never let me take my son. My son belongs to him. Everything belongs to him. I belong to him. He'd never have permitted me to leave, but I managed to escape while he was on one of his pilgrimages." Her expression went cunning. "He's very religious now, Hope. After a few years of being worshiped he began to take his religion very seriously."

"So he's religious," I said, which was certainly not the worst offense I'd ever heard of a man committing. "You knew he had a touch of fanaticism when you met him. That's what brought you two together." Then the full implication of her statement dawned on me. "You mean Babi doesn't know you've left Ustan?"

"Not yet he doesn't. He didn't know I'd kept my American passport."

Again the self-congratulatory look of cunning swept over her slightly swollen features.

"Was that very smart?" I said. "Leaving like that without making a few sensible arrangements?"

"I had to leave like this," she said, her voice dropping a register or two as if the place might be bugged. "I'm pregnant, Hope." She put her hands on the belly concealed in the folds of her green skirt. "Pregnant with another of the monster's possessions. I had to leave quickly before he found out, or he would hold me captive there forever."

I was stunned, stricken, subdued in all possible ways by my successor's tragic fertility.

At first I didn't identify the ringing in the room as the doorbell. I thought it was merely the heart-stopping whine bombs make as they drop on their targets. Joanne almost hit the ceiling and huddled into a ball, her head covered, as if she were protecting herself from an invasion of henchmen come to force her back to Ustan.

I was glad to put some distance between us. I started toward the entry, and Joanne skittered after me. "Please don't tell Libby about . . . you know." She folded her arms protectively over her belly.

"She'll have to know sooner or later."

"Maybe not," Joanne pleaded, and then slipped off into the pit-of-pits. I'd forgotten about the kettle, which was glowing red-hot, the water long since vaporized. I had to turn off the flame and refill the caldron before letting Libby in, so naturally, she was livid by the time I opened up.

"Better late than never," I greeted her.

"Hope, I'm so sorry to be so late. I was detained." She was breathing as if she'd run a marathon. She staggered into the foyer and then almost strangled herself in a furious effort to pull her voluminous poncho over her head. "Is Joanne here?" Her good manners continued to operate through the plastic tent.

I waited to be sure she'd survive the struggle before answering. "What exactly do you mean, 'detained,' Libby?" And then I got a glimpse of her catatonic daze. "Detained by a pack of mesmerists?"

Joanne emerged from the water closet looking remarkably recovered, and why shouldn't she now that she'd given me her troubles to brood over? "Libby," she sang out in her melodious

"You don't want to hear any more, do you?" Joanne shyly understood.

"Hear any more of what?" Libby's paranoia ignited.

"We've been talking about the breakup of my marriage." Joanne quietly satisfied Libby's quest for knowledge. "I should have told you sooner. Forgive me, Libby, but somehow I couldn't. Not till I'd spoken to Hope." She gave me a regal nod. "I've left Bahram, Libby, left him forever. I'm never going back to him."

"No!" Libby waved her sandwich around. "You haven't left him. It's impossible. Only yesterday at lunch you showed me the pictures and described the paradise of Ustan, and you were happy. What has Hope been saying to you?" She jumped up and glared at me. "Has she been filling you with her vile negativity? Don't listen to her. Don't let her spoil your happiness!"

I was bowled over by this tribute to my powers of persuasion. Even Joanne was thrown off her riveting delivery. "It has nothing to do with Hope. What a strange idea. Hope has been so kind to me, listening to me. I have been miserable, Libby, terribly, horribly. Can't you see it? It's written all over me, isn't it? The truth is impossible to hide."

"But you wrote to me, beautiful letters," the nitwit persisted. "I read them. I even read them to Hope, every happy word of them, didn't I, Hope?" She beamed at me from across the table. It occurred to me that Libby's two inhabitants, the skinny one and the fat one, were locked in combat for control of her fragile psyche. I didn't care. I was already operating on overload.

"I was trying to be happy, Libby. Trying my best to make the marriage work. But the harder I've tried, the more he's come to abuse me."

"Abuse!" I heatedly objected. "You're not going to accuse him of being a wife beater, too, are you, Joanne?" Her assassination of Babi's gentle character truly stung me.

"Dear Joanne. How awful. And me going on and on about how happy you were. Our lunch must have been a torture for you." Libby averted her eyes from the suffering centerpiece to transfer her wrath to me. "Why don't you believe her when she says Babi has been abusive? She should know. She was there, not you. Why don't you ever accept anything you're told? People can find themselves in miserable predicaments not of their own making. Why, I found myself in one only today." She slapped her palm over her mouth to shut the crimson thing up. Then she sank to the tufted seat of her wing-tipped throne and cowered there, a big red bag of bones. "It was so awful, so humiliating." Her spread fingers hid her face. "I'm never ever going to Bendel's again as long as I live. I understand exactly what you're feeling, Joanne, when you say you'll never go back to Babi."

A silence thick as a mist descended on the Three Witches of Endor. We all sat there, cooking our private stews. Mine was ready first.

"What were you doing in Bendel's today? Did you completely forget about your appointment with Joanne?"

"You see," Libby shrieked, struggling to an upright position, "you see what I mean? Now she's going to find fault with me, make me the guilty party, when in fact I was doing it all for you, Joanne. I'd arrived at the Tea Room with half an hour to kill"—she flashed me a superior look—"so I dropped into Bendel's, which is practically next door, because I thought how nice it would be to pick up a surprise for you, something frivolous, decorative, a luxury. You did seem so sort of sober yesterday. I did notice, but I didn't want to comment. I wanted to help. But she"—an accusing talon was aimed at me—"she'll twist everything around and try to prove I was doing something wrong and Bendel's was right when they claimed I wasn't buying their manufacturer's copy of an original Italian knit, but was stealing the ridiculous item." Anguish shook her gaunt form. "It was so insulting, so humiliating. I could have died of shame. I should sue them for shock. But they wouldn't believe me either"—her reproach was directed at me—"no matter how often I explained to them that I had simply taken the vest out to the street to check the shade in natural daylight. Their fluorescent lighting is a crime." She swallowed hard at the word. "Well, it is! It turns any color into mud. And maybe I walked two steps up Fifty-seventh Street to see if you might be waiting in front of the Tea Room, and these two ordinary, very housewife-style ladies came charging after me, identified themselves as store detectives, and ordered me to reenter Bendel's." By now her moans were following a regular rhythmic beat.

"You were checking a color outside Bendel's in this torrential downpour?" I expressed some curiosity.

"They have awnings," she challenged me.

I decided it was wiser to get the whole story before dismembering it. "What did the lady detectives do to you?"

"Hope, it was horrible! They took me downstairs to a cubbyhole in Bendel's cellar where they cross-examine everyone they catch shoplifting." She groaned and was perilously close to an attack of hyperventilation. Joanne and I exchanged concerned glances. "They had the nerve to make me empty my pouch on a desktop, and they took the liberty of looking through every item in it. And the strangest predicament developed because this pouch is so small it holds hardly anything. It certainly couldn't hold my billfold, which I'd left on my dresser, so I had no identification with me, and when they asked for a phone number, well, I figured I wasn't home, so I gave them yours, and when they asked me my address, of course, I gave it, and in fact, in all the confusion, I might even have mistakenly given them your name."

Vertigo seized me.

"Hope, I'm positive it won't matter. Nothing further will

happen, I promise you. And if they try to make any trouble, I swear we'll sue them for false arrest. I'll even call on one of the family lawyers. I shouldn't have mentioned the incident. It's too silly, upsetting you over nothing. Enough about me." She took a violent puff of her cigarette. "Joanne, dear, why don't we move the party up to my place and let Hope get some rest? She looks tired."

"You gave them my name?" I couldn't recognize my own voice. My deep dread of legal authorities constricted my throat.

"This brings back such personal memories," Joanne shyly intervened. She rose from her easy chair and posed at the hearth, the better to capture our attention. "I can't help remembering the old days when Bahram and I and our whole group appropriated store property as a revolutionary tactic. We were so naïve, so idealistic. Imagine trying to fight the values of this materialistic destructive society by such peaceful means." Her features went soft and tender. "Bahram and I were so close then, a team. I'd do the boosting, and he'd be the lookout. We didn't care what we took as long as there was no profit for the capitalist pigs." She was moved to chortle at the antiquated terminology. "I still believe we were politically correct, in principle. Bahram continues to despise the attachment to material goods, particularly as it is practiced in the West, the lust for equipment and conveniences, expendables that are wasting the planet's energy reserves, impoverishing all of the Third World, destroying the future in the guise of progress." She concentrated her brilliance on my enraptured landlady. Libby was studiously oblivious to my stricken presence in my own living room. For how long? "Thank you, Libby." Joanne's visage was the mask of tragedy. "It was thoughtful and kind of you to want to cheer me, but ornaments do not cheer me. They do the opposite. I've lived too long now with women crazed by greed and acquisition. Women maddened by their need to shine as ornaments, proud to display their husband's thievery on their own vain backs. They're too ignorant to understand

that these ornaments they covet are the chains of their own op-
pression."

"Libby," I cried when Joanne came up for air, "what do you
mean you gave them my name?" I knew I sounded peculiar,
but I was making sounds, wasn't I? Not from the reception my
pronouncement received, I wasn't.

"Then it's just as well they took the vest back." Libby never
disengaged from her exchange with her best friend. "And I
couldn't agree with you more, Joanne, especially the part about
madness. It's marvelous how clearly you put things. That's exactly what happens. One is crazed trying to keep abreast of fashion. My goodness, one day everything has to be skintight, and
the next we're expected to costume ourselves like parachutists.
Isn't that so, Hope? Hope knows what I mean," my landlady
continued to commune with Joanne. "I'm forever giving her
items that are perfect in the store and completely old hat by the
time I get them home. It drives me mad, the colors, the shapes,
the changing lengths. Let's go." She jumped out of her arm-
chair. "I can tell when Hope has had it." The beast loved me
from a safe distance. "Don't look so tragic," she scolded me.
"No one is coming here to haul you off to jail." Libby had recovered her bonhomie at a remarkable clip. "It's not too late
for lunch, and I'm still famished."

Joanne consulted her plain windup wristwatch and frowned
at what she saw. "It's getting rather late," she commented,
"and I did want to get to a rental agency before five. I can't stay
at the hotel. I absolutely can't afford it."

"Won't Babi take care of all that?" Libby went all practical.

"I don't want his money. I don't want to be his property any
more. I'll manage on my own. I have my wedding pearls, and
they're fairly valuable. And as soon as I'm settled, I'll find gain-
ful employment, and one day"—her voice dropped to a rum-
bling murmur—"I'll get my son away from the tyrant."

"You're a marvel, Joanne, and of course you'll manage.
We'll help you to manage, Hope and I, won't we, Hope?" She

gave me the friendliest of nods, to which I made no response. All I cared about was that the duo was leaving at last. It was almost too good to be true.

"So we'll have lunch another day, Libby. I must make finding a place my first priority."

I saw it coming. Even with my eyes closed, I saw it coming.

"But, Joanne, there's room for you here."

"Here?" I cried in desperation, but I knew I had no power to alter the awful consequences so cunningly set into motion by the scheming marvel.

"You can move into Stuart's apartment." Libby disregarded me. "He never uses the place. I don't know when he's planning to come back. Of course, it's his, I have to hold it for him, but if I wanted to put a friend in there for a short while, he'd be glad for it to be of some use. Oh, please, Joanne, you must move into Stuart's." Libby coaxed her, oblivious to the lack of resistance her offer had provoked.

"Libby, do you mean it? Do you really mean it? I could live here with you and Hope, my two closest, my two only friends, almost. Oh, Libby, you're an angel. You're a saint. You are the most generous human being I've ever had the good fortune to know."

The two buddies waltzed, arm in arm, into the foyer. I felt as though I were falling into a bottomless well. Down, down my spirits plummeted. My perilous fall was accompanied by a scream from Libby.

"Hope, you've let the water boil out again. You are destroying my valuable and irreplaceable kettle." With that final blow, they were gone, but not for long.

By nightfall Joanne was moved in, bag and baggage. From below I could hear the clumping and scraping and shrieks of girlish laughter. What wouldn't I have given to awaken from this nightmare to resume my normal pauper existence?

6

Common wisdom has it that we never know when we're well-off! Fool that I am, it took Joanne's commandeering the parlor floor for the profundity of that adage to sink in. It was hell from the word *go*. On the morning following her installation above me, she came pounding at my door to invite herself in for breakfast, eager, as she put it, to talk. *Talk* seemed to be her motto, though *diatribe* would have been more accurate. Despite all my efforts to stem the slander, she compulsively filled me in on Babi's unforgivable offenses. I passively listened to the shrew, hardly able to keep my eyes open. His worst offense, so far as I could make out, was that instead of inciting a peasant rebellion, his fiery spouse sharing the command, he preferred to spend his days beautifying his estate and elevating his mind. He was also guilty of being born into the rich and ruling family of an underdeveloped country, another sin I could find in my heart to forgive. The princess detested her in-laws. Babi's parents were both dead, but there were a couple of married older sisters and their spoiled, useless offspring, plus an uncountable number of uncles, aunts, and cousins, as families composed of a dedicated husband and a dozen or so assorted wives tend to be large. This patriarchal system had only recently been outlawed by the present emir of Ustan, who had at the same time prohibited women from wearing the traditional veil, as it was his aspiration to be in step with the powers of the Western world. The prince's obedience to the ambitious emir, a despot as well as the biggest pig amongst his many uncles, had revealed her husband to be the weakling, the hypocrite, the craven parasite from whom Joanne had fled.

I let her ramble on, her courteous captive audience. The sin of sins, the offense Joanne could hardly articulate without turning into La Pasionaria, was the prince's neglect, his indifference, his cruel disregard of her needs. Joanne's needs! Litany without end. She needed respect, purpose, equality, love. What she also needed was an abortion, and that, too, was the fault of the prince. How could she gratify his masculine ego already swollen to corrupt proportions by producing another child? Yet the fetus within her was part of her own body, over which she was determined to recover her rights! Was the abortion a free act or a reaction to Babi's tyrannical control? I wanted to scream at all her hair splitting. I was one hundred percent convinced she was not going through with the birth, whether her motive was revenge against the prince or disenchantment with motherhood, or she'd still be in Ustan, doing so in luxury. Her face pinched and sad, she finally stopped the pros and cons of the matter and asked if I knew of an abortion clinic, which I did not. I advised her to check the back pages of the *Village Voice.*

That topic exhausted, she segued into the steps she should take to launch herself on a meaningful career. Did I have any helpful suggestions? As if I didn't have a few problems of my own to resolve without her becoming my central obsession.

Joanne and Libby had a date to go sight-seeing and then, of course, lunch that first afternoon. There were so many places the princess wanted to visit—a discount drugstore; an army-navy surplus store; an organic food store; and a feminist bookstore she used to haunt. Has anyone ever heard a more alluring list of entertainments to make a princess storm the snake pit?

A few hours after their raucous departure, the two old friends gyrating in a frenzy of togetherness, they returned, and I, secreted behind the geisha screen, got the full measure of the privacy and serenity I might never again have the luxury of taking for granted. Every move they made, every word uttered, every cup rattled, every single solitary sound resonated loud and clear through my low tin-pressed ceiling, as if I were jammed inside a speaker wired to the stage above.

Another knock on my door. This time it was Libby, her plucked features contorted with worry. Joanne was sick, good and sick—fever, body aches, the works. What should *we* do? I explained that I did not have a license to practice medicine, though that detail would have posed no obstacle, as Libby presently called on her personal acupuncturist, Mr. Li, one of her miracle healers.

In the week of illness that followed, Libby raced around like a maniac, beating a nonstop path to Joanne's sickroom, delivering papers and magazines, herb teas, vegetable broths, an upright lamp, fresh sheets, more towels, another pillow, and so on. She had not a moment's rest from her ministrations. I suggested getting Joanne's mother, who was a registered nurse, on the case, but Joanne passionately vetoed that practical solution. Mr. Li was doing a marvelous job. He was a genius, and even more important, Joanne revealed sotto voce, he knew she was pregnant, as Libby still did not, and as soon as she was stronger, he was going to healthfully abort her with his magic needles and miraculous herbs. I'd never heard a crazier plan. Had she flown halfway around the world to the fount of modern medicine in order to submit herself to some exotic mumbo jumbo? But Joanne had become so infatuated with the wisdom of the East even its rickshaw runners had to be as gods! I personally would be only too happy to have the Great Wall of China rebuilt, only twenty feet higher than the original, and a similar structure thrown around India.

Back and forth Libby ran, nursing her patient, her gaunt face martyred, the hallways ringing with their voices as they left the doors ajar lest Joanne be stricken with a need! Stuart's telephone had been disconnected, but soon Libby attended to that, too. Without warning, my landlady would barge in on me to accuse me of being no help at all.

My only respite came with the long nights when the rest of the household slept, but the release I craved and required was invaded by woeful memories of the stupid fashion in which I'd deprived myself of a prince. Joanne's return had loosed a Pandora's box of buried incidents that now played themselves out, vivid as hallucinations, in my suffering mind. The time I'd locked him in the hall—I could hear him banging on the door and pleading for entry. The time I'd tossed his essential drugs out of a fifth-floor window. The time I'd let him fester in the Tombs for a whole week before condescending to bail him out. The memories were as blows against my heart, awakening remorse, regrets that had been accumulating in it for six years. How had my anger grown as foolish and vengeful as the anger expressed by Joanne? What had I been trying to prove? If I could only see him, sit with him, have one of our all-night incomparable marathons that always cleared the air and brought us closer. I pictured my Babi alone in Ustan, the space beside him vacated, a space fate might have reserved for me. I was reduced to writing my former and only husband a few simpleton letters in my illegible scrawl, reporting, of course, on Joanne's presence in the house but focusing on my constant concern for him and imploring a prompt response.

I made a few neighborly sick calls on the invalid upstairs. I couldn't remember the last time I'd surveyed the perpetually locked parlor floor. What potential for gracious living it offered, with its fifteen-foot-high ceilings and soft light coming through the front French windows and a real rear door opening onto a railed porch with a wooden stairway descending into the verdant garden that *could* have been.

Joanne could be found on a mattress pushed flush against one of the cracked and flaking walls, a lobster crate functioning as a bedside table, surrounded by an ever-growing accumulation of teacups and broth bowls and magazines cast aside on the broad planks of the sagging floor. Unlike my den below, the vast space was devoid of furnishings, nothing but a bentwood coat-tree in one corner, the princess's modest wardrobe hanging from its swirling antlers, and an assortment of giant floor cushions for the comfort and convenience of her guests. I'd pull one of the big pillows closer to her pallet and keep her company for a while, inquiring, after a decent interval, if she'd heard from the prince. *I* certainly hadn't. She always delivered the same negative reply plus her assurances that he was still on his pilgrimage. Was the pilgrim pumping his way to Mecca and back to Ustan on a skateboard? Joanne's happiest moments were when she had both Libby and me solicitously in attendance. By the second or third week of her residency she was well on the road to recovery, and, it developed, she had not just been lying there on the floor concerned only with herself.

"Libby," she announced one day as my landlady was conscientiously fluffing up her pillow, "it's a pity the way you're letting this house fall into ruin. Aren't you planning to ever fix the house?"

My landlady sat back on her heels, her gaunt face wary. "Of course I am. I've had a hundred architects look over the place, haven't I, Hope?"

I had rarely in my life had less desire to speak.

"You have to stop deceiving yourself," Joanne scolded her. "That's an avoidance ploy, not a genuine decision to act. Look at these walls; they're buckling—it's a hazard, Libby. And the floors! They could be so magnificent—oak floors, what could be more elegant?—and they're so pitted and uneven you could break your neck."

"Well, it's Stuart's place . . ." my landlady prevaricated, but with no success.

"Stuart has never lived here a single day," Joanne fondly berated her best friend. "He's only an excuse for your habit of letting everything slide."

I watched my landlady's erect back stiffen. Was I also watching the end of a beautiful friendship?

"Both you and Hope seem to think I'm made of money. If

you heard the prices quoted to me just for applying a coat of paint!"

"If you can't afford to take care of it, you should sell it." Joanne had no end of sensible suggestions. "It's so depressing to see anything this perfect be destroyed by sheer negligence. Even Bahram"—she paused and remembered to look hurt— "who truly disapproves of ostentation and display, has been renovating the palace. These historical landmarks are not only personal property, they belong to all of us. They are a source of pride, a credit to mankind's positive capacities. Maybe you should consider donating the building to the city. It could be a museum or a nursing home."

Libby bestirred herself. She stood up and smoothed wrinkles from the front of her sack dress. It was clear that Joanne's well-intended criticism had much more authority than my pauper complaints. "I have an appointment for a float at the tranquillity tanks." She icily excused herself and marched out of the room.

"I hope I haven't offended her." Joanne turned an innocent visage on me. "It's for her own good, really. These French windows don't close, they can't be locked—it's dangerous! And the wiring, Hope—every time you use your hair dryer, my lamp dims and the refrigerator breaks down. This house could go up like a tinderbox."

"Tell me," I said.

Joanne's full recovery consigned me to the lowest circle of hell, torture that should have come as no surprise. At the slightest sign of life from the lower depths, down the inside stairway the troll would hurtle, eager for communion. Libby had more or less walked off the job and was incommunicado in her gutted tower, so I endured the full impact of Joanne's *need* for female companionship. It had been the worst of her many Caspian deprivations, the lack of an intelligent woman she could share her thoughts with. A sister. She repeated *ad nau-*

seam how much it meant to her to be located in such nurturing proximity to a mature and experienced woman. Different as our temperaments were, there was so much we could learn from each other, wasn't there? I hid from her insatiable wish to learn, to share. I crawled around my cramped quarters like a thief, an army deserter, but our apartments were too acoustically joined for me to escape her sharp surveillance. If the coast was clear and she didn't intercept me leaving the house, she caught me on my return, ready and eager to deliver the latest thrilling progress report on her quest for independence. She was beginning to feel like a person again, and look like one, too, thanks to the amazing benefits of a brush cut, no deeper than an inch, that hugged her scalp like a glorious coat of fur. It was also my impression, if creaking floors do not lie, that Mr. Li was sticking more than needles into the paragon.

And still no word from the prince. His silence was an unmitigated source of punishment. Did I no longer exist for him? Had he wiped the slate clean of all his American wives? Had he merged my identity with Joanne's and drowned the tasteful package in the Bosporus Sea as one of his renowned ancestors periodically had done when he grew tired of his noisy harem?

I fled the deteriorating convent as often as I could, and more often than not there was nowhere to flee but to Marshall Springer's loft. He was not lavish with the sympathy. Joanne had been raising my consciousness for more than a month when I found myself dining Chez Marshall.

It was an ordeal to consume one of my mentor's home-cooked specials. It's uncanny what such an intelligent person can do to ordinary food. Eggs turn watery; meats become plastic; chickens stay raw and all but cluck after hours in his malfunctioning oven.

"It's a Michael Field recipe." Marshall was civilizing me.

"Is that right? Didn't he die?"

My host's slitty Mongol eyes, set deep under heavy brows,

went slittier. He screwed up his Russian peasant face, with its wide cheekbones and broad nose and bushy mustache. His dark brown hair was sticking straight up from the toil of cooking.

"You're really a hoot to have around lately."

"Excuse me for not being more fun. It's just that I haven't slept in five, going on six weeks."

"On the contrary, Hope, you've done nothing but sleep. You're breaking all records."

"Says who." I toyed with a piece of gray matter on my plate. "Did you know Florence Nightingale took to her bed for fifty years when she returned from nursing the wounded in the Crimea? It's a fact. Tell me, Marshall, do you think Florence was actually asleep or only hiding from her adoring public, and how do I convince Joanne I am not her nurse and don't want any more of her adoration?"

Marshall carried the dessert from the oven to the table. The dining table was a desk, all of his important papers shoved to one side. We were seated on swivel chairs, the type that tilt back and disgorge you if you forget yourself and relax.

"For someone who stood out in the rain getting sick rather than disturb my rest, it's amazing how Her Highness has come to feel entitled to my constant assistance. Today it was the cleaner's. Would I mind accepting their delivery, since she had a more important appointment at NYU to take a battery of aptitude tests? She's still undecided where she can do the most harm."

Marshall wasn't even listening to me. "Shit," he said, "the crust didn't cook. It shouldn't be all doughy like this, should it, Hope?"

I averted my gaze. The pie filling was exactly the same consistency and color as the blighted main course.

He sampled his creation. "It tastes better than it looks."

"I'm not in the mood to eat hot apple pie," I said with tact.

"It's not a pie, dummy. It's a cobbler. An apple cobbler.

Can't you tell the difference? What were you brought up in, a stable?"

I laughed. He knew very well where I was brought up. Marshall and I dated from way back, where we lived as children in semidetached villas on the shores of Brooklyn. His mother, Natalie, was a distant cousin of my mother, Betty, increasingly distant now that Betty Diamond has gone to her Eternal Nap. Natalie was napping, too, in Sarasota, Florida, using up every penny of her dead husband's insurance policy.

"Let's take a walk. I'll treat you to an ice cream cone at David's," I offered.

Marshall sampled some more of his creation while a roach crawled over the edge of the pan to do likewise.

"Let's get out of here," I moaned, and we did.

We climbed down five rickety flights of unlit stairs and came out into the perpetual carnival of the East Village. St. Mark's Place was one continuous bazaar of ethnic merchandise. In front of the shops, on cloths spread over the sidewalk, our new indigent population were offering a peculiar assortment of wares—rusted safety pins, moth-eaten sweaters, cracked phonograph records, unmatching shoes, and other similar finds. The stoops were filled with junkies on the nod, who I liked to think were too weak to be dangerous. This particular locale made me feel peculiarly dated because the kids and the style they had adopted—all punk and high nostalgia for clothes that had been fashionable enough yesterday—were definitely another generation that evinced not the slightest interest in my adult and old-fashioned presence. It was a new style, not mine, to take everything, especially themselves, as a great big post-Holocaust joke. Heads shaved, arms tattooed, rag-doll girls with hand-painted eyelashes and Betty Boop lips, teetering over in their mother's hysterically funny high-heeled shoes. Marshall loped beside me in a costume I wasn't too crazy about either— farmer-in-the-dell overalls on top of a sleeveless orange T-shirt and, on his big feet, basketball Keds. For the president of Hadassah, he was remarkably indifferent to his sex-object rating.

We turned downtown on University Place and walked along the outer edges of Washington Square Park. It was a lot cooler outside than it had been in Marshall's place, and impoverished hordes with no air conditioners, such as myself, were taking advantage of the breezes the park supplied. I never penetrated the park any more. Parks, I guess, had become the property of the street people. Anything you couldn't lock up was the property of the street people. Anything you didn't hold onto good and tight was the property of the street people. It was very invigorating to stay so constantly on the alert.

Marshall puffed contentedly on his menthol cigarette as we continued past the private gardens of the high-rise south of Washington Square. The other side of Houston Street was the start of SoHo. SoHo hadn't yet boomed during my Babi reign. Now West Broadway, the main drag, was all spanking-new galleries and boutiques that were also pushing ugly, but at real high prices. We window-browsed our way down to Canal and stopped at David's street counter to get containers of egg creams.

"I have just one thing to say," I said as I finished my soda and added the empty container to a roadblock of garbage.

He gave me a suspicious look.

"If Babi isn't dead and isn't blind and hasn't had his wicked hands chopped off, why hasn't he written to me?"

Marshall pulled a cigarette from between his lips. He did not conceal his annoyance. We had an understanding: If I brought up the topic of the prince again, he'd shoot me. I had stuck to the agreement all through the inedible dinner.

"Babi is not your problem. He's Joanne's husband. Let her worry about him. And that's it, Hope, end of discussion." He flicked the butt onto the sidewalk and ground it under the sole of his sneaker.

"That's why I haven't heard a word from him? Because he's Joanne's husband, not mine? He hasn't been my husband for more than five years, but he's always been a diligent correspondent."

"He has not," Marshall irritably retorted. "There's nothing unusual in your not hearing from him for a month. As long as one of your medical emergencies didn't arise, his silences never seemed to bother you, so knock it off, Hope."

"But under these circumstances?"

Marshall gave me a ferocious look.

"I'm sorry. I'm worried about him. Do you mind if I feel some concern for the only man who's ever taken any responsibility for my well-being? If I could afford it, if Babi had taken more responsibility, I'd be on the next flight to Ustan to assuage my fears. Would you believe it, Marshall, the only thing preventing my mercy mission is a few lousy bucks. You don't happen to have two thousand dollars you could spare?"

"I wish I did! I'd love to ship you over there and be rid of you once and for all. How long do you think you'd last in that Arab camp? You'd open your big Jewish mouth, and you'd be sifting through the sand dunes for your molars."

Politics! The bane of my existence.

"I'm writing an interesting piece on Lubitsch's pre-Hollywood comedies," Marshall apprised me as we waited for the light to change across from the twin towers.

"Terrific. The world must be holding its breath." I smiled at him. He didn't smile back.

"It keeps me busy. You know, sweetheart, it wouldn't be such a bad idea if you found work worthy of your talents. Imagine, you could be something besides an unemployed *femme fatale.*"

That was all I needed. A pep talk on how I should give purpose to my slothful life by taking a job away from some deserving man. "Once and for all, Marshall, accept the fact that I'm not an achiever. I'm an appreciator. There has to be someone at whose feet accomplishments can be placed, and I have contributed mine."

He snickered as we wandered under the sculpture big as the prow of a ship on the corner of the World Trade Center. I really like it down there. There are hardly ever any people around, and the spacious plaza at the center of those high, high buildings makes me feel as if I've escaped from the city.

"If that precious prince of yours hadn't entered the picture when he did, you'd be a hell of a lot better off right now. You'd just done a really great makeup job on Michael's revue."

"I had not. Please stop reviving that rumor. Any moron could have done it better, or at least as bad. Do me a favor, Marshall, get off my back and go be Joanne's guidance counselor. She's another one I'd like to get off my back."

We'd entered the vast esplanade, and I was thrilled to discover, if nothing else, at least the fountain was working. Waves of water roared out of the base of a revolving globe in the center of the fountain and then spread like surf on the flat platform to run off the edges like a waterfall. The water sounded great, and I was instantly one hundred percent cooler. We took our places side by side on one of the cement banquettes to enjoy the show. Marshall took a tightly rolled reefer out of his bib pocket. He drew in a powerful lungful of smoke and, still choking it down, passed the joint to me.

"How are things going with Joanne?" He exhaled the question in a stream of smoke.

"Would you like her phone number?" I asked him. He took the joint back from me and sucked on it again. The burning tip flared and sputtered in the dark air.

"Has she had her abortion yet? I keep forgetting to ask you."

"Oh, sure, she must have had it a couple of weeks ago, as soon as she was ambulatory again."

"The acupuncture method worked?" He was understandably astounded.

"I doubt it. I assume she ended up at a clinic with the rest of the riffraff. She didn't give me the gory details because she probably wants me to think Mr. Li's nightly visits are professional, the tart."

"Did the abortion throw her into a depression?" Marshall always took on this lugubrious tone on the rare occasions that he addressed himself to female functions. Every now and then I have to remind myself my mentor wouldn't touch one of my gender with a ten-foot Torah.

"Not in the slightest. She's just the old obnoxious, opinionated, exhilarated Joanne. It's Libby you should be worrying about. She's the one who's depressed. She never leaves the house till the wee hours of the dawn. Sometimes I catch a glimpse of her sneaking down the front stoop on a commando raid, and she slips back in, carting these armloads of groceries. It's such a ghastly sight I don't have the heart to stop her and talk some sense into her."

"What a crew," Marshall allowed with a satisfied chuckle. He passed me the joint. I inhaled the pungent fumes till the remains of the joint burned my fingertips, and I dropped it fast. I leaned back and gazed up at the ribbons of lighted windows that turned the sky-high buildings into floating space stations. The lights made shimmering patterns in the agitated surface of the water. A wave of melancholy hit me and pulled me into a powerful current.

"You know, I was pregnant with Babi's child, too," I said, and my chest almost caved in with the saying. "Why didn't I have it? How could I have been so stupid?" My sadness was as strong as a chemical injected into my system.

"You didn't have it because you're not totally irresponsible," Marshall told me.

"Oh. Is that why?"

"How long did you know Babi when he knocked you up? A few months? Furthermore, you had the good sense to realize you weren't mother material."

His composure, his certainty, made me want to hit him.

"How did you get so all-knowing? Maybe I could have been a fantastic mother. It might have been the Messiah I aborted. And you helped me! You delivered me to that butcher! I'm sorry," I said quickly when I made out his face in the darkness. "I just go out of control when I realize what a mess I've made out of my life. What is it with me that I can't hold on to anything?"

"Hope"—he actually took my hand—"stop beating up on yourself. You are who you are, a lone, a solitary diamond. You were not meant to be surrounded with little baguettes. Only a crazy Arab, and a virginal one to boot, would have the audacity to imagine he could claim Hope Diamond for himself."

"Well, I don't know about that," I said, allowing for the exaggeration marijuana provoked in my spiritual adviser. "True, I was awfully young, too young to understand I was dealing with a once-in-a-lifetime opportunity. How old was I? Twenty? Twenty-one?"

"That's a pretty close fit. Why don't you try twenty-four, twenty-five for size?"

"Are you crazy?" I hollered. "I was only twenty-four, twenty-five when we married, and we'd already lived together for a good four years."

Marshall lit one of his menthols and sprawled along the cement backrest.

"Listen, toots," he said in a greasy voice, "I can make the mathematics of your heartbreaking youth real simple. You met Babi approximately ten years ago, a date I well remember, because to my undying regret, I dragged you to the mixer at International House when you spotted and zeroed in on the poor bastard. Babi was a retarded twenty at the time, a recent escapee from a Swiss military school, and putty in your experienced hands. Is it possible you are confusing your age with his age, back then, which would be an understandable error and could in fact account for the five-year discrepancy we seem to be disputing?"

"God, you get pedantic when you smoke dope," I said.

Marshall slapped his thigh and got carried away in gales of drugged laughter. He took a few deep breaths to recover control and wiped his wet eyes. "You know, Hope, Babi didn't look like much then. He wasn't a bad-looking guy but, let's face it, in the runt department—delicate, beautiful, but not an irresistible hunk. I've always wondered how you smelled it out that he was a prince."

"I was genuinely attracted to him, Marshall. You and I do not share similar tastes, I am happy to say. I was not on the hunt for a title. And believe me when I tell you that in bed Babi very quickly demonstrated that he was heir to a thousand years of harem intrigue. He was bliss! He didn't have even a concept of normal."

Marshall laughed.

"What am I trying to prove? I lived with him for four years, and then we married. It was obviously more than a pickup!"

"True," Marshall conceded, "true. It was one of the great romances of the twentieth century."

"It was a marriage! And Babi was the best, the kindest. It was the only time in my life I wasn't entirely alone."

He shook his big, bushy head solemnly. "I should say not. There were always at least twenty stoned-out junkies crashing in your pad."

I couldn't take another second of his smart-ass voice competing with the roar of the fountain. I jumped up. "Let's start back."

He stayed seated for a while, busy calculating on his fingers. "Listen to me, see if you can follow this, Hope. If you knew how old you were now, and if you subtracted ten from that figure, you would, I know it's hard to believe, get the age you were ten years ago when you met the prince. Now—this is where it gets a little complicated—if you added four to that sum, you'd get the age you were when the nuptials were held at City Hall five or six years ago. The figure I come up with is very close to thirty, but enough, I don't want to bore you with a lot of statistics and technical stuff. Let's go."

"Have you ever considered the damage marijuana has done to your brain?" I demanded as we started the trek back.

Marshall just laughed and had himself a ball all the way home.

We stopped in front of the house, leaning on the gate, and smoked a final cigarette. It was part of our ritual. There were no lights lit on Joanne's floor—it was way past her bedtime, at least midnight. A sliver of light showed through Miss Haversham's curtains on the top floor. I didn't feel like going inside anyway, not alone.

"Come in for a nightcap," I urged him.

"I'd prefer to cap my night somewhere else, Hope."

"Marshall, am I always going to end up alone?"

"To be continued, Hope," he said with a brotherly hug, and I watched for a minute till he vanished around the corner.

7

And so another perfect week of my perfect life lurched by, highlighted by the morning appearance of the stooped mailman pushing his three-wheeled cart down Grove Street and invariably doomed by the letter, the pardon, the release from the prince that was never granted. I suffered. I withdrew deeper into my private world of regret. The days of this world were lived inside out. The midnight creaks of Joanne's mattress were my all-clear, my signal to come out of hiding, take a bath, make coffee, call Marshall, live my life. I would stay up till the mail-man delivered my daily bout with frustration, and then, with the stirrings of breakfast activities reverberating from above, I would crawl behind the screen, unplug the telly, douse the lights, take the phone off the hook, and lie upon my catafalque in wide-eyed exhaustion. The state of our union did not please Joanne, and when she caught me, she'd expostulate loud and clear on the disappointments, the failure of our support system, with neither Libby nor me cooperating. At least in Ustan, bad as it had been, there was a bustling household around her. She had my sympathy.

It was around five o'clock in the afternoon, and I was busy playing hide-and-go-seek with Joanne, wondering how I could sneak out of the house for a constitutional, when my phone rang. It was the hour Marshall sometimes called in the hopes of dispatching his duties then and not at three in the morning.

"Hi," I laconically spoke into the receiver.

"So I finally got hold of you" were his opening words. "I've been trying to get through for over a week. I was getting ready to send in the cops. Hope? This is Leo," he said, "Leo Her-mann." As if I hadn't recognized his voice from the first syllable.

"Yes, Leo, I know it's you," I answered in my new sepulchral tones.

"You sound weak. Is anything the matter? Are you sick?"

"I'm in excellent health, Leo. Why are you calling? I asked you last time not to call any more." Leo had not walked out of my life without a backward glance.

"I can't hear you," he said. "Do we have a bad connection? What is this business of leaving your phone off the hook all the time? What's going on down there?"

"I need to be left undisturbed," I said.

"Hope, wait, don't hang up. There's something I want to ask you."

"Make it snappy."

"Can you have dinner with me tonight?"

Dinner? Though the afternoons had been mine, his evenings belonged to Muriel and the business he ran to keep her in furs.

"No, I can't," I said.

"Why such a quick no? There have been a couple of changes that might influence your answer."

"I told you, Leo, I'm busy. I can't permit my concentration to be broken."

I was as attentive to the upstairs movements as a sentry guarding a fortress under siege.

"Muriel and I have separated," he swiftly inserted into the conversation.

"No kidding!"

"It's been nothing to kid about. The woman has been driving me up the wall. Believe me, I was more than glad when the marriage counselor advised a trial separation."

"A trial," I purred, amused in spite of myself. "I'm not sure I've ever had dinner with a man on trial. You're just allowed to walk around like a free person?"

"Hope, please, I'm not in the mood to make jokes about my situation. Just come to dinner at Leopold's, and if you're interested, I'll tell you the whole story."

Leopold's? My suitor's restaurant has been strictly off limits, also in consideration of Muriel.

Joanne's toilet flushed. An air bubble lodged in the pipes boomed as if I'd sustained a direct hit.

"What was that explosion?" Even Leo heard it from wherever he was calling.

"It's nothing. My ceiling just collapsed."

"So what do you say, Hope? I'll send a car for you at seven, and we'll have a nice, quiet dinner at Leopold's."

"You'd send a car for me?"

"I'd send a golden coach," he offered, in a rare flight of fancy.

I laughed and reached for the last Vantage in the crumpled pack.

"Wonderful. I'm so looking forward to seeing you and talking to you, Hope. I've thought a lot about what you said to me, how you felt I'd acted. A lot. I promise you there'll be a few pleasant surprises." Leo pushed his luck, so to speak, and hung up without allowing me time for an argument.

To be honest, the prospect of some social distraction had its appeal. Muriel and Leo separated? I pulled myself out of my pothole of a mattress. The news sort of rocked me, which was silly, when I thought it over in the tub, because after all, what's so unusual about an essentially dull marriage not surviving the loss of a nonmeddling mistress?

After my bath I blow-dried my hair and did my face and finally ransacked the mirrored wardrobe for a knock-him-dead outfit. What to wear to Leopold's was not an irrelevant question. The place was very casual and yet very style-conscious. Though the basic American fare was reputedly quite good, it was not for food that Leo's celebrity patrons packed the premises. They were there to be numbered among the elite of chic achievers, which was another consideration to compute in selecting the appropriate attire. They certainly didn't want to look like a pack of hicks at an awards dinner; no, they wanted to look as though they were unaware of ceaselessly celebrating their success. *Casual* was the watchword, and so I settled on a charcoal gray silk jersey ankle-length T-shirt that would have had Carlo Ponti storming the divorce courts and was also amazingly crease-free. I slipped my bare feet into a pair of high-heeled strap sandals that were designed not for walking but for being fetched by limousines.

The driver must have been waiting outside, parked at the curb, because at precisely seven the doorbell rang, and this hulking kid in jeans and a City College sweat shirt asked me, while wiping his nose, if I was ready. It was a warm night, but I still felt more secure taking the black fringed shawl along. I know how you can freeze to death in the back of those air-conditioned stretch limousines. The chauffeur, who introduced himself as Sherman, led me to a station wagon and opened the front door to allow me to arrange myself in the passenger seat, while he got behind the wheel. It was all just as it had to be, as the back of the station wagon was piled high with all kinds of boxes and cartons that I vaguely thought might be the personal property Leo had moved out of his and Muriel's Central Park West co-op. Leo's gofer turned out to be the boss's nephew, of all things, and when he wasn't carting fair maid around, he was studying to be a business administrator, though what he really wanted was to be a matinee idol, and all the way uptown he treated me to his Humphrey Bogart imitation.

Humphrey went off to park the station wagon, and I tottered through the door of Leopold's, into a delightful blast of ice-cold air. The long oak bar up front was hopping, three deep, as this was actually Leopold's cocktail hour, way too early for dinner. Rush, of all nonentities, was one of the bar crowd, leaning lasciviously over a young woman who I didn't pay any attention to, except to notice that she had short, curly hair and a rather plain, piggy face.

Leo was at my side in an instant. He took both my hands in his and, in full view of the bar, gave me one of his bear hugs. "You're an angel to come up here. You look like a million dollars, Hope." He never let go of me as he led me to the dining rooms in the back of his dark, wood-paneled, wooden-floored, old-fashioned-looking restaurant. The walls on either side of the back room were lined with red leather banquettes behind oblong tables set for two. There were big round tables taking up the center aisles, their crisp white tablecloths set for larger parties. The place was illuminated by low-hanging frosted globes, and there were no silly plants and none of those annoying sacramental candles in the middle of each table.

We sat way in the back, in the furthest reaches of the second dining room, and there was only one other couple across from us, exchanging soft endearments. A waiter in a black waiter suit and a white shirt and black bow tie ran right over to pull out the end table, and I slipped onto the banquette, Leo slipping in after me. He took my shawl and placed it on a ledge behind our heads. There was a small square ribboned box conspicuously propped up in the center of my place setting. I looked at everything but it. I even took a good look at Leo. For a man on trial, he was in high spirits. His china blue eyes were crinkling from the nonstop smiles on his seamy, familiar face.

"Aren't you going to ask me what's in the box?" he gaily teased me.

"Oh." I looked down at it with all the shock of discovery I could muster. "This box?"

Leo laughed. "Open it," he urged me, and then to the waiter who'd never moved away: "Jimmy, bring out the bottle of Heidsieck, the one back there in the bucket I've been chilling."

"Champagne," I drawled at him. "What are we celebrating?"

"I don't know about you, Hope, but I am celebrating my freedom, my new life. Today I am a man," he said with a chuckle.

"And what were you yesterday?" I flirted with him.

"Yesterday I was a condemned husband. Let me tell you, there's quite a difference. The accusations I've had to listen to, the attacks, the hostility. As if it was so easy for me to have her locked up under house arrest—a wonderful role model for Cynthia, a mother who's too frightened to get down to the lobby."

The ribbons were off the box, and I lifted the top to behold a crystal pendant watch, lying inside a delicate pool of gold that unraveled into a long, thin gold chain.

"Leo, it's beautiful!"

"You like it? You really like it?"

"I love it. It's so delicate, so exquisite." He was helping me hang it 'round my neck. "I swear," I gurgled, "I never knew you had such good taste or I'd have been a lot madder at you."

I lifted the ornament off my chest and studied the tiny face with its spidery numerals and spidery hands magnified under the crystal. The windup stem was set with a tiny sapphire. "I don't know what to say," I said.

"Try 'thank you,' " he suggested, with one of his paternal pats.

But as it developed, I could not get those words out of my mouth, and so I leaned over and kissed him on the cheek, which he seemed to find equally acceptable.

The waiter—boy, was he handsome—had uncorked the champagne and was filling our two wide-lipped glasses.

"To our new, unencumbered relationship." Leo contributed the toast. We both drank to it, though I was not quite sure what he had in mind. "Are you hungry? Should we order now?" He solicited my wishes. "I usually eat a pretty early dinner because the place gets too packed later on."

"That's fine with me if we eat now," I graciously consented.

"What do you feel like eating?"

"I don't really know. What would you recommend?" I felt the smooth crystal between my fingertips.

"Have the loin chops. We serve the best lamb in New York—the real thing, milk-fed. I get them shipped in from a ranch in Montana."

I mentally conjured up the slightly gamy taste of lamb. I concentrated on the decision. "What about your filet mignon? How does Mimi Sheraton rate it?"

"She ran out of stars," he assured me.

"Then I think maybe I will take the lamb chops." I sipped contentedly at the cold bubbly. A party of six or seven big shots filed into the back room, and one of them waved to my dinner companion.

"Excuse me a second, darling," Leo said, and he squirmed off the bench. "Lamb chops for two," he dispatched the waiter, and then went over to greet his customer-friend, who I suspected might be Norman Mailer. The two men were about the same height and had the same graying mop of ringlets. He gave Leo a few fond punches and then grabbed him in a friendly half nelson.

"Is that Norman Mailer?" I excitedly asked when Leo returned. "The one standing next to the red-haired giantess?"

"Shhhh," he said.

"If it is, that's who you really resemble, much more than Paul Newman. You could be brothers, twins."

"Shhhh," Leo said once more. "I didn't force you up here to notice other men."

I laughed, of course, and downed the rest of my drink. I had a refill before the glass hit the tablecloth. "Really, what was your motive?" I asked coquettishly.

"I have only one motive, Hope"—he suddenly went serious and fixed me with a level gaze—"and that is to please you, to prove to you I can be a *mensch,* not just some poor bastard on a treadmill who's cheating on his wife."

I was more than glad that our food arrived at that propitious moment. The charred lamb chops were curved around broiled mushroom caps, with little pleated skirts on the tips of their little snapped-off ankles that killed what I thought was my appetite. The waiter came charging back with the side dishes, a big platter of steaming crisp-crusted home fries, a Leopold's legend, and a bowl of freshly prepared coleslaw, which also enjoyed legendary status. Jimmy extracted a bottle of red wine clamped under his arm, flashed the label at Leo, and, receiving a subtle nod of approval, poured the red wine into two balloon glasses and then respectfully backed off, leaving the bottle on the table. I was sad to see the champagne go and promptly consoled myself with the red wine.

Leo sawed into his lamb chop and, finding it done to his satisfaction, instructed me to eat. "Mmm, these are perfect. Taste yours, darling."

I took a teeny-weeny nibble.

"Is yours good?" he inquired before I could swallow.

"Delicious."

"Is it cooked the way you like it? Is it too rare?"

"It's perfect." I watched the blood ooze out onto the mushrooms.

"It should be perfect. They charge an arm and a leg for these loins."

"Leo, they're so perfect that when they take the electric chair out of mothballs, these definitely should be a last meal."

His bright blue eyes checked me out with a sidelong motion. "You have a very unique mode of expression, Hope." I sensed a not-so-undercurrent of displeasure. Leo was making me very nervous. It wasn't the same at all as seeing him in my Grove Street rut. I had also had enough of his exhilaration for the moment.

"Is Muriel as happy as you are about the separation?" I asked, concentrating on the potatoes, which were great.

Leo set down his fork and knife on either side of his plate. "I tell you this in all objectivity, Hope. The woman has lost her senses. How long has it been since I've seen you, six, seven weeks? In that brief period I witnessed a transformation that was like watching Dr. Jekyll become Mr. Hyde, if you know what I mean."

I clucked.

"It began on the trip to Africa," he filled me in. "If I said to her, 'Muriel, I hear there's a very beautiful lake in a bird sanctuary an hour from here, should we go take a look?' she'd answer, 'I want you to stop controlling me!' " He shrugged his compassionate shrug.

I clucked some more. I drank some more. Fortunately, I didn't have to smile some more.

"I was as patient as any man could be. I've been patient for twelve years, why should I stop being patient now?"

"Good point," I said by way of encouragement. I must

admit, I rather enjoyed hearing the details of the breakup. I drank some more wine and decided I was having a good time. More bar customers were drifting back to dining tables to eat, and they all genuflected before Leo. It certainly didn't feel like a bad place to me. Rush had no doubt walked Miss Piggy down to Alfredo's to splurge on the pasta special. Was Miss Piggy his wife? What was her name? I cut the thought short.

"I'm not a brute." Leo stood his palms up on his chest. "I understood, or I tried to understand, what it means to a person to get back their courage, their feelings of confidence after twelve excruciating years. Not that she didn't seem to be a happy woman, Hope. Don't get me wrong. She loved her house. She loved her child." He pursed his lips together. "And it was my mistake to think she also loved me. She was a very contented, sweet-tempered, fulfilled woman. I gave her everything she wanted or asked for. She knew I forgave her for her incapacity. And anyway, it's amazing how people can compensate. She put all of her energies into her house and her family. It was enough for her."

I filled my glass myself.

"Slow down on the wine, sweetheart." He lifted his brows at me and then resumed his narration. "So naturally, I encouraged her, I supported her efforts. Do I want Cynthia to grow up believing that when she's a wife and mother, she has to become a prisoner?" He frowned. "The only thing I can't forgive Muriel for is her indifference to the effect all this shake-up is having on Cynthia. You know how kids blame themselves for their parents' separation and get stuck with all the guilt." He stared at me in an intent fashion that demanded an immediate confirmation.

"I wouldn't worry too much about Cynthia," I said, exuding the comfort, the solace women are so often called upon to produce from their bosoms. "Teenagers are pretty resilient. When I was her age, I used to beg my parents on bended knees, 'Please, please split up,' and to tell you the truth, if I had any guilt, it was that I always felt they stayed together to spite me, and in the end it didn't do either of them any good."

Leo just sat there, half-turned to me on the banquette, as if new worlds were opening before his eyes. After a long pause he spoke. "I never think of you as someone who had parents."

"I should be so lucky." I speared a piece of potato to go with my refill of wine.

"Are they alive?"

"Who?"

"Your parents. Who are we talking about?"

"Well, we were talking about Cynthia and Muriel and how patient and forgiving you are, and well, that was as far as you got."

"What more is there to say? You do the best you can. There's nothing under the sun I can do to change the fact that she was confined to the house for twelve years and I was relatively free." He gave me a self-effacing smile. "If she hates me for that and can't forgive me, and nothing else will do but for her to be with a twenty-six-year-old emotional cripple who also hadn't left his bedroom for twelve years, I throw up my arms in defeat, and I have to say, 'All right, Muriel, go right ahead and wreck your life.'" He chugalugged his glass of wine. "Her loss can be your gain, Hope," he said, and he picked up his napkin and patted his stained lips. "What do you want for dessert, kid? We have the best mousse in the world."

A feeling that could have been anger rose in the very same bosom that stored all my solace and comfort.

"Leo, I haven't been at home praying you'd leave your wife."

"Don't jump down my throat if I put something a little awkwardly, Hope. All I meant is that this gives us the opportunity to find out what we really feel for each other." He did the pouring this time.

"Gee whiz, Leo, you're really into trials, aren't you? Is that allowed, to have two trials going simultaneously?"

"Shhhh," he said.

There was no question about it. It was anger all right. "Stop shushing me! I am not your wife."

"You're twisting every word that comes out of my mouth." He gave me a look that accused me of twisting a far more sensitive organ.

"Let me make myself clear. It was never my dream to step into Muriel's shoes, to be her understudy. What I wanted, all I wanted was to be a luxury, a treasure, a treat. . . ." I couldn't spend all night explaining myself to him. I thought how enjoyable it might be to push over the table.

"What do you think I'm suggesting, that you scrub my floors?" He laid his hand over mine. "That's what was so marvelous with you, Hope. You were a treat. You were the biggest luxury I ever gave myself." He was stroking my fingers, interlocking them with his, his clear blue eyes reassuring me. "In a couple of weeks it will be August."

"No!" I said.

"What no?"

"It's that close to August?" No wonder it was so hot out there.

"Pay attention, Hope. Stop playing with that watch and chain for a minute." He gave the tabletop a couple of quick raps. "I always close Leopold's for the month of August."

"Is that a fact?" I felt my lips pull into a prim smile.

"How would you like to join me on a first-class luxury cruise around the beauties and antiquities of the Greek isles?" He was giddy at the rare pleasure being offered to the likes of me! "The least you have coming to you is a trip."

"I'll think about it, Leo."

His tender lips tightened. "You'll think about it? What is there to think about? I'll show you a fantastic time."

I sank my eyes into his. "Thank you. I told you I'd think about it." Funny how easily I got *those* thanks out.

Leo sighed.

"Why don't you just be good to yourself and say yes? Are you afraid I'll spoil you so much you might get to like it?" His hand under the table was squeezing my thigh. The waiter rolled a cart of pastries at us. "Try the key lime pie," Leo advised, now patting the thigh he'd been stroking. "You'll love it. Give my beautiful guest a piece of the key lime pie," he ordered the gold-skinned Adonis. A wedge of green meringue was flourished before me. It surely was restful to have someone else doing my thinking. "Snap out of it, darling," Leo said, and put an arm around me. "I feel like getting out of here." He put his mouth close to my ear. "I feel like being a bad boy and taking the night off. Let's go somewhere and have a good time." His thumb moved along my jawline.

"I'm having a good time here." I checked the good time I was having as magnified through the rock crystal of my pendant watch.

He pulled himself together, put my shawl over his arm, and the waiter was there pulling out the table and celebrities were waving and I put on my public smile and we made a gracious exit.

"Where are we going?" I promptly demanded, taking my stand on the sweltering street.

"We'll go over to the Plaza, okay?" Outside his kingdom Leo went slightly timid, and the hand clutching mine was nervous and a bit damp.

"What's at the Plaza?"

"My temporary quarters," he said, going sheepish. "Paramount always keeps a suite there, and Bob insisted I use it."

He waited on tenterhooks for my consent. What the hell, I was rejecting a month on the Greek isles; I could spare him a night at the Plaza.

"Well, the price is right," I said, and looped arms with him as he hailed a Checker.

We entered the suite and went through a narrow pantry to

get to a main room as spacious as Stuart's parlor. There were some modern paintings on the wall, all very hard-edged, but the rest of the furnishings and the walls and the carpets were a symphony in beige. There was a cranky Feder's huffing and puffing on the sill of a deep, tall beige-draped window, and it felt more like a fan than anything refrigerated.

"Wow," I said, flopping on the beige couch, "Paramount must be hurting."

Leo was opening and closing cabinet doors in the recessed pantry just off the entrance. He came toward me, bobbing on the balls of his feet, jauntily juggling a square crystal decanter containing booze.

"Are you trying to make me drunk?" I gave him a very disapproving look.

Leo laughed. He put the decanter on a beige marble coffee table that held a few beige ashtrays and a beige copy of *The New Yorker*. He sat on the other end of the couch, and he picked up my feet, one at a time, and slipped off my punishing sandals. He pressed his thumbs into my aching soles. "Ah, you devil," I said, "you know my worst spots."

"Funny how tastes can differ, isn't it?" He chuckled at me and kept his hands moving till they found another terrible spot.

"You really have no right to do that," I told him, my head resting on the arm of the couch.

"I won't do it very long, I promise," he pampered me.

"Good," I said. The room turned gently around me as if I were being rocked in a cradle. I felt as though gravity had been fighting me for days and days and had finally given up. Leo pulled me up by my hips and helped me out of my truly sensational T-shirt gown. He rubbed his hands over my breasts, and I could feel him feeling how fabulous my skin felt.

"I'd better get you into a bed," he said gravely, and I hardly opened my eyes as Leo assisted me across the carpeted floor.

I fell backwards on the bed, dressed only in my new watch

and chain. Leo, stripping off his own clothes, came and sat at a corner of this orgy-sized let's-make-a-deal bed. Just imagining how many sexual negotiations were thrashed out here made me almost achingly hot. Or was it Leo's clever hands, dissolving everything they touched? He tried to slip my watch and chain off me, but I held onto it and said, "Keep your hands off my valuables!"

"Oh, God," he said, and pressed his head on my chest. "What you put me through, Hope. You just make me jump through these fiery hoops of yours. I'm so burnt-out by the time you give in, I'm here as your helpless slave."

I giggled and ruffled his hair. I always had a good time with Leo in bed. He was so good at it you really didn't mind turning over the controls.

"Why do you have to get the better of me all the time, Hope? Are you afraid you're going to want so much? You have to keep me in my place, here, below you. . . ." And damned if he didn't get below me.

"Don't be so proud of yourself, Leo," I told him, and scratched his scalp and opened up to the yearning that had accumulated in me from all the days past, of all the mailman's rotten trips, and listening to Joanne and not being wife material or mother material or any material except the material I was being now under Leo's expert ministrations.

Leo was not beside me when I awoke in this strange room, with muffled sounds coming from the street a mile down. The strange room was filled with a beige light, which made all my surroundings look powdered.

Leo came dancing into the room, wrapped in a big bath towel, his hair wet but towel-dried, his face clean-shaven. He smelled of soap. He sat down right next to me and slipped his thigh under my head. "Did you have a good time?" he asked with a sly leer.

"I don't remember a thing," I said.

Leo laughed and gave me a flat, soft slap on my bare bottom.

"What time is it? Why are we running out of here like this?" I didn't feel like moving.

"It's early, Hope, way before your wake-up time, and mine, too, but I've got to get an early start today."

"How early?" I was looking at my watch. Through the crystal I read ten to six.

"Well, it's a three-hour drive to Cynthia's camp. And I want to be there by eleven." Cynthia the remarkable was summering at a Weight Watchers' camp.

"I didn't know you were going to visit her today."

"Muriel and I have been splitting visits, and one of us goes up every other weekend. We don't want Cynthia to feel that because we've separated, we've separated from her."

"You're a wonderful person," I told him. "But nevertheless, you don't have to start out on your trip at six o'clock just to be sure you arrive before eleven." I sat up and pulled the sheets over my breasts.

"What's this six o'clock?" Leo checked the Rolex on his wrist. "It's after eight. We've got to move it, Hope." And he busily pulled on his jockey shorts.

I checked my watch again. It still said ten to six. Hadn't we been talking a couple of minutes? I held the watch to my ear. Nothing. I looked at its small mechanism through the crystal back. Nothing was moving. None of the little hammers were hammering. None of the tiny spoked wheels were turning.

"Leo!" I screamed. "It's broken." I felt the way I felt when I was six years old and broke my brand-new doll's brand-new head.

He jumped and turned around, radiating alarm. "What's the matter, Hope?"

"It's broken. I broke it! You were right. You should have taken it from me. I must have smothered it during the night."

"What is this hysteria?" He held his temples as if I were giving him a headache. He moved cautiously toward me till he saw the watch lying flat on the palm of my outstretched hand.

"Oh, for God's sake, a fuss that almost gave me a heart attack over a piece of machinery. The dealer who got it for me said if there was any malfunctioning, not to worry, he'd take it back and do the repairs."

I stared at him, hardly making sense of his words. "You knew? You knew you were giving me a busted watch?"

"It isn't busted," he groaned. "Stop acting like a child. These old things sometimes need work done to them. Come on, Hope, I'm not a jeweler. I'll take care of it tomorrow when I get back."

I transferred the trinket from my palm to his. "Here," I said, "here's your broken watch." And I moved fast into the white tile bathroom with its big white fixtures and stood under as cold a shower as I could take, pressing a cold washcloth to my eyes until I felt presentable enough to face my public. I went right to the satin chair beside the bed and took my T-shirt and pulled it over my head. I got into my sandals with no delay, grabbed my shawl, and said, "I'm ready to leave, Leo."

We waited in a long, wide corridor for the elevator in front of doors that could have been filched from St. Patrick's. I watched the arrow moving around a half-moon, and when it stopped at seven, the cathedral doors opened.

Cabs were lined up at the steps of the Plaza. We realized we were going in opposite directions, me downtown to Grove and Leo uptown to his garage in the West Seventies. He put me into the first cab and told the driver where to take me.

"I'll be back by tomorrow night. I'll call you. Think about August, promise." I nodded my head. The driver took off. Somehow, in the sweet sorrow of parting, Leo forgot to give me cab fare; and I forgot that I'd forgotten to put mad money in my bag, so all the way home I was glued to the mounting figure on the meter and kept counting my nickels and dimes and checking to see if I'd make it.

8

We were parked in front of Grove Street, me feeding coins into the hackie's saffron palm, when a scream disturbed our slow count.

"Hold that taxi!" It was Libby on the steps of the brownstone, loaded down with a big, sausage-shaped duffel bag and a big weekend case, ponchos flung over her arm.

"Where in the world are you going?" I asked her as I came crouching through the open door onto the curb.

"Hope! Where have you been? I gave up trying to reach you." She clutched her own throat, and her features behind wraparound glasses impenetrable as a blindfold went all sneaky and paranoid. "Are you coming from the hospital?"

"What? What would I be doing at a hospital?" I pressed my back against the door and was ready to take my stand there forever. The driver stepped on the gas. Libby had a fit.

"I told you to wait!" she barked at him, and about five generations of robber barons were in her commanding tone. The driver simmered down and got positively meek. "You can put my bags in the trunk," she added.

"I don't have all day, lady." He grumbled out the one and only English phrase he had committed to memory and did as he was ordered.

"Oh, Hope, something terrible has happened. An accident." Libby's features were clenched in shock.

I couldn't have gotten a word out if I tried.

"Joanne is in the hospital. St. Vincent's. The police took her there. A neighbor noticed her lying on the top step, *unconscious!*" Her voice went dog-whistle high.

This time I tried to speak and couldn't.

"The house hit her!" Libby wasn't trying to get past me any more but stood, robot-still, making her announcement.

"The house hit Joanne?"

"A piece of it. A big piece of it from the cornice, up there." She pointed straight up, and as I lifted my eyes to the roof, she moved fast, belly-crawling into the rear of the cab. She fell back on the plastic seat and sprawled there. "Hope! Criminal charges could be brought against me, for negligence!" Again the screech of the needle sliding off the record.

"Libby, where are you going?"

She didn't answer me. "La Guardia," she boomed at the driver, who was back behind the wheel, and then to me: "I'm going to Stuart's, on the Cape. Goody advised me to leave." Goody was the family retainer, the one who'd have attended to my shoplifting arrest. "Hope"—she grabbed my wrist and lowered her voice—"oh, Hope, why did she ever come here? It was so good without her. Get rid of her, and you can have the whole downstairs. Don't let her sue me! Talk to her; she'll listen to you." With that she released my wrist, and while I rubbed the aching spot, the cab pulled slowly away from the curb. Libby stuck her frizzy head out of the window. "What are you doing out at this hour in a Halston!" she cried as the cab picked up speed and zoomed off, burning rubber.

What *was* I doing out on the street at that hour in an ankle-length Halston? I whipped down the three shallow steps and let myself in. The quietness of the building hit me as if a piece were falling on me, too. I could hardly tolerate being there for the time it took me to pull off my fineries. I got into black pants and a T-shirt and stuck my feet into a pair of black flats. I streaked out of the building and couldn't keep my walk down to a run till I reached St. Vincent's.

A volunteer in the main lobby took her sweet time till she found Joanne's card noted with the room number. It was nine o'clock on the electric wall clock above her desk, visiting hours were in progress, and I pushed with the pack into a freight-sized elevator. I raced along the glassy corridors, gagging at the overpowering stench of disinfectant, and came to a full stop only when I was smack in front of Joanne's bed. There were four white iron beds filling the four corners of the pale green hospital room. Hers was closest to the door.

"Hope, isn't this a bit early for you to be making calls?"

Thank God she could speak! She was sitting at the edge of her high crib, her legs dangling over the iron sides, her head cocooned in a helmet of gauze, dressed for the street.

I had to hold onto the bedpost to steady myself.

"Did you just find out about the injuries I sustained despite my repeated warnings to that menace?"

I had never seen Joanne more agitated.

"Do you realize it was a miracle I wasn't killed? As it is, they've given me a series of encephalograms, and they're not sure there isn't a concussion or a cerebral clot." She fired these technicalities at me. "We'll know in a couple of weeks. Till then I'll be staying with my mother."

"Your mother?" My lips were shaking.

"She is my closest kin and had to be contacted in case brain surgery was indicated."

"Oh, my God," I said, and sank down onto a white metal chair at her feet.

"I'm waiting for Mother now." Joanne seemed somewhat mollified by my speechless horror. "She's at Grove Street, packing up my things."

I nodded rapidly.

Inside the gigantic cotton bathing cap Joanne's Pekingese features compressed into a fist. "I told Mother not to come here till she called Uncle Roy, who is a top insurance lawyer, and instructed him to start proceedings against Libby. If this is what she wanted, a battered victim on her doorstep, well, she got it, except this victim is fed up with indulged, privileged, useless, cruel people acting as if it were their God-given right to set themselves up above the rest of us and squash us like worms, like bugs under their selfish, heartless feet!"

I reeled at the rage the injury had set loose in Joanne.

A nurse intervened. "Kindly do not disturb the patient!" she rebuked me, glaring at me through frameless hexagonal glasses.

I promised to try. "You see, Joanne, the nurse is right. You shouldn't let yourself get so overwrought. How is your head? Does it hurt?"

Oblivion from Joanne. "I warned her, you were there when I begged her to take responsibility for her property. You can be my witness. It could have been you as easily as me lying there unconscious!"

A part of me wished it had. "Joanne," I said, "what satisfaction can you get out of suing Libby? She won't face the music, though she should. The Strauses will just hire a slew of lawyers, and they'll fight it out. No, no, it will cause you more trouble than it's worth to sue Libby."

"I'll see to it the destructive parasite is forced to have her day in court." She repeatedly stabbed a forefinger into the flesh of her thigh.

I buried my face in my hands. The consequences of Joanne's righteous wrath were self-evident to me. The Straus Corporation would board up the house and send Libby somewhere to improve her skiing, and I would find myself with a shopping cart for an address. "Joanne, she was only trying to be generous. She took you in out of kindness. It's not as if she herself couldn't have been the one lying on the stoop."

"The fact that she may have an unconscious wish to end her empty life does not mean I have to pay the price. Who the hell do they think they are, up there? No, Hope, we have to learn to fight, or they will annihilate us. You're afraid you can't survive without Libby's charity"—she let me have it right in the face—"but I thought the same about Bahram. How am I going to live? How will I survive? But we will survive—and more than survive." She tenderly cradled her stomach in her arms. "I almost lost the baby," she said in a hushed whisper.

"What baby?" I stupidly said.

She smiled with a ghoulish and ghastly pride. "My baby. I never aborted it. It wouldn't let go, Hope. Mr. Li said he never treated a fetus that hung on with such strength, such tenacity. This is no ordinary child. This is a fighter inside me, and it has held on again and given me some of its strength to fight the persecution I have endured in their households!"

"Joanne, is this true what you're telling me?" Was it the raving of a person with a concussion? She hadn't alluded to the pregnancy for a month at least.

"I'm sorry it comes as such a surprise to you, Hope, but I had to keep my decision secret." She paused and wistfully tilted her grotesque head. "I was afraid you might try to talk me out of it, the way you tried to do with my Abbas."

We might have stayed there, locked in that mute tableau for eternity, if Joanne's mother had not bustled in. She was small and neat and gray-haired and efficient and ideally suited to the hospital ambiance.

We'd never met before, and with that formality concluded, she enlisted me to help Joanne off the bed and arranged for her to totter between us, supporting herself on our linked arms, her big, white, hairless head wobbling like the oversized head of an infant. I further assisted the princess into her mother's car and was cordially offered a lift home. I said I needed a walk.

The pedestrian scene on Seventh Avenue was Sunday-morning sparse, except for a spontaneously organized convention of beggars and loons, hitting on me every step of the way. I felt like one of them, mumbling out loud. I even caught myself throwing my arms around in the air, convincing God-knows-who of God-knows-what. It was a small miracle I didn't join the desperate parade and keep walking and talking and flailing about for the remainder of my destitute days.

I tried not to see the rubble mixed with chunks of mortar

scattered on the front stoop as I slipped into my endangered shelter. I do not know how it came to pass that my next moves were so smooth as to be preordained. Perhaps a Higher Force was guiding me. Without missing a beat, I marched to the rear of the apartment, knelt at the prayer rug behind the geisha screen, rolled it up into a tight tube, clamped it under my arm, and marched it out of the house, onto the street, and directly to the Persian Rug and Carpet Shop on the corner of Christopher Street, which I prayed would be open for the Village invasion of Sunday tourists.

"I have a rug to sell," I told the proprietor, a large young man with five o'clock shadow, though it had to be hours till noon. We'd met in the past, but I wasn't at all sure he'd remember me. His name was Hossein, and he had been Babi's fellow student in those woebegone college days.

"Show me the rug," he said politely, and he wasted no time asking for a sales slip or any proof of ownership. He spread the small carpet on a bare, bleached floor and pensively gazed down at it, scratching his shadow.

"Do you remember me, Hossein?" I brightly asked. "I remember you. It's been a long time, seven or eight years probably, but I used to go out with an Ustanian student—in fact, we were married. . . ." I was talking a mile a minute, and my smiling jaws felt as though a dentist had stretched my mouth open with iron clamps.

His liquid brown eyes remained politely blank.

"His name was Bahram, Prince Bahram—do you remember him? And my name is Hope, Princess Hope if you want to get formal." I laughed for him. "This rug was a wedding present from the emir of Ustan, so it must be valuable."

"Of course I remember," and I could see that he did. He became more like a person and less like a foreigner. "How is my old friend Bahram?" He had, of course, formerly groveled before Babi's royal person.

"I'll know soon," I told him. "I'm going to Ustan, and I thought I could always pick up a couple of new rugs there, so I might as well sell this one and buy lots of American goodies like jeans and stereo parts—I don't have to tell you how welcome those things are there." I took a breath that all but lifted the rug off the wooden floor.

"An excellent idea," he assured me, and started a slow promenade around the rug, which looked cheaper and dirtier and crummier to me, lying there in the midst of platforms of gorgeous carpets, not to speak of more brilliantly hued rugs hung like tapestries on the white walls.

"This a beautiful shop you've fixed up here." I deepened our intimacy. "I love those plants. Is business good?"

"I have no complaints." He mildly put any fears I might be harboring to rest. "And how valuable, Hope, if I may call you Hope"—we consented with our eyes—"how much money do you expect for your rug?"

"Two thousand dollars," I blurted out before my mounting panic could drop the price. He didn't fall over in a faint or break into gales of hilarity. He kept rubbing his chin while circling the shrinking carpet.

"Two thousand dollars is a quite proper value for you to place on this rug. Do you have any other similar items at home?"

I knew then that poor Libby was really getting screwed.

"I might," I said. "I'll take a look around." I wanted this transaction to move right along, and if it took him fantasizing that every Sunday I'd let him steal another treasure, so be it.

He rubbed his palms together. "Could I offer you a cup of coffee? I make it myself there in the back of the store."

"I'm afraid I don't have the time."

"Then we will finish our business quickly," he said, carefully rerolling the rug and managing to make it disappear. I followed him to a desk in the rear and watched as he opened one of those extra-big, five-checks-to-a-page commercial check-books.

"Oh, no! No!" I cried, as if he were ripping off my clothes. "It has to be in cash. It has to be in American dollars. All of it. No cash, no sale. I can't take a check."

"But I do not have that amount of cash here. How could I, with the muggers and the thieves up and down Bleecker Street from morning till night? I would have my throat cut."

"Give me back my rug," I yelled.

He winced. "Do not be so hasty. We will try to arrange something. Perhaps my wife, Nan, could bring the cash which is kept at home, to the store."

"Call her now," I ordered. And he did. Within half an hour, as I sipped a second nerve-jangling extract of coffee, Nan, an American frump pushing an infant in a baby stroller, arrived and withdrew an envelope from under her precious child's seat. She handed it to her husband, who counted and re-counted and counted for a final time before offering it to me, apologetically admitting it was $100 short, but truly all the cash they had at home. He threw in a twenty from his own billfold and showed me that he was depleted of all possible resources.

I took the money and ran. I ran back to Grove Street. I pushed the envelope under my mattress and lay on top of it, my body pumping so much adrenaline into my system I could taste it on my tongue.

When my breathing and heartbeat became more normal, in this mortuary of a house, I drank a big glass of water, took another to the phone, and dialed a number I had dialed before, just as a dress rehearsal for the real performace.

"Pan American Airlines, good morning." A friendly female voice greeted me.

"Good morning to you, too. It is a nice morning, isn't it?" Silence.

"I want a ticket on the next flight to Ustan."

"Excuse me?" she said, and I had to repeat myself. "One

moment, please." She put me on hold. After an eternity she got back on. "There is no direct Pan Am flight to Ustan, but there is a stopover in Ustan scheduled on flight number two."

"Is that the next flight? You don't have anything else going sooner?"

"Madam, this flight is scheduled to depart Kennedy Airport this evening at nine p.m."

"Is there a seat available?"

She made me wait all over again. Ommmmmmmm, ommmmmmmm, ommmmmmmmm, I chanted to myself during the endless seconds.

"There is a seat available," she reported back to me.

"I'll take it," I said, without waiting for another word.

"Will you be going first or economy class?" she pressed on.

I couldn't drag out this exchange, not if I was leaving tonight. "I have two thousand dollars to spend," I told her.

My candor actually provoked a chuckle out of the automaton. "Oh, then you most certainly will be traveling economy class. That will be one-way economy class?"

"You tell me," I hollered.

"We do have an excellently priced package deal if it would interest you, with an open date of return after a minimum period of forty-five days."

"I'll take it," I said again.

The rapidity of the sale was too much for her to handle. "The price of the economy package comes to fifteen hundred dollars and forty-eight cents, plus a three-dollar departure charge, bringing the total to fifteen hundred and three dollars and forty-eight cents. You could, if you wished, arrange your return reservations at this time, or the arrangements can be made from your future point of departure."

"Please," I begged her, "don't give me a flying lesson. Just give me the ticket!"

A pocket of dead silence filled my ear. Had she hung up on me?

"I'm sorry," I breathlessly poured into the receiver's little black perforations, "really sorry. I didn't mean to be rude. I'm just in a terrible state at the moment because I've received word that my husband is lost on an archaeological mission on the Caspian, and I am frantic with worry."

"Oh, I'm so sorry to hear that. I quite understand your distress. Unfortunately, not all of our passengers are traveling for pleasure." It was the most human sound she'd made thus far. "Could I have your name, please?"

I told her.

"Is your passport in order, Mrs. Diamond?" At first I didn't realize her question was directed at me.

"Yes," I said, "of course." Was it? Where was it? I hadn't seen it since flying back from Haiti after my disastrous divorce.

"And how will you be paying for the ticket?"

"In cash."

"We can hold your reservation for one seat on flight two till two hours before flight time. Our offices in Manhattan close at noon on Sunday. Will it be possible for you to pick up your ticket at Kennedy no later than seven p.m., Mrs. Diamond?"

"Yes," I said, and said no more.

"Then I will confirm your reservation now on Pan Am flight number two, leaving Kennedy at nine p.m., Sunday, July thirteenth, arriving Hetron Airport, Ustan, Monday, July fourteenth, at six-fifteen p.m. local time. May I on behalf of Pan Am wish you a very pleasant flight and, Mrs. Diamond, a very successful flight, with my personal wishes that you will quickly locate your husband."

That last part was really sweet of her to throw in.

I made another call, lest it slip my mind, this one to Western Union. I chuckled as I spelled out my message. What a kick he'd get out of it!

ARRIVING HETRON AIRPORT 6:15 P.M. BASTILLE DAY.
VIVE LA REVOLUTION. LOVE, HOPE.

Now for the niggling issue of the passport. I opened the miniature brass pirate's chest that holds my legal identity and a few photographs of the people I used to know best. I paused over a photo of the two of them standing before a snappy Packard, him in a houndstooth jacket and dark slacks, looking so debonair, a loose arm capturing her shoulders, a Lucky Strike drooping from careless fingers, and she, dainty as a heroine on the silent screen, looking straight at the camera, straight at me, with her sad, unseeing eyes.

The darling passport was right where it was supposed to be, not even at the very bottom, and I checked the dates, counting on my fingers. It was valid, valid through September, which would be our fifth divorce anniversary, five years as blank as every single page in the book except the first. And now—to mark the next with its last and most important stamp.

A factor I had recently suspected turned out to be true. I did not own a suitcase. I thought of going to the prince with nothing but the clothes on my back, but then again, there's a limit to symbolism. I pulled the envelope out of its safekeeping and counted out $1,620. I pocketed the remaining $300 and dragged myself out into the heat for an inescapable last-minute bit of shopping on Orchard Street, where the merchants were as observant of Sunday as the Ustanian rug stealer. I hailed a taxi and zipped over to Orchard and Grand. The place was hopping, an unruly mob of looters gone wild.

In my weakened state I allowed a wigged old *bubba* to shame me into buying a thirty-nine-inch, genuine cowhide, steel-framed, brass-buckled valise with an equally square, equally genuine cowhide vanity case for a measly 150 breast-beating dollars. God should strike her dead if the big valise alone didn't sell for $400 plus tax—which she was willing to forgo—all along Fifth Avenue.

It took but two steps from her narrow alley of a shop for the dead weight of my purchase to make it shudderingly clear that the wily old harridan had outwitted my Higher Forces. Half dragging, half carrying the colossus, I elbowed and shoved my way down to a pushcart piled high with a rainbow array of panties and bras under attack by the Furies. Since underwear was going to be an essential aspect of my relocation, I joined in the fray and dug in, grabbing whatever they let me reach, handicapped by the necessity of straddling my giant suitcase. I almost keeled over when the skinny, bearded peddler in black suit and hat to match magnanimously rounded out the price to $50.

Nothing was going to make me part with the remaining C-note until, and this was unplanned, I had reached the end of the block and was searching anxiously for an unoccupied taxi when my roving eyes accidentally lighted on a rollaway coatrack jammed with merchandise offered at a 50 percent discount. I had to satisfy my curiosity. What should I find hanging in the midst of rags you couldn't sell on St. Mark's Place but a navy blue pure linen classical shirtdress, with a button-down collar and a hem shaped like shirttails, created for continent hopping. The original price tag from Saks was dangling from a small pearl cuff button, and the garment, which had sold for a daunting $160, was slashed to $80, and trust me, the greedy owner was unable to stick me with paying his taxes.

Rain was starting to fall as I scored for a taxi. The streets went into pandemonium, as if everyone were caught under enemy fire, and did I feel lucky to be whisked away from that bloody scene. As will happen, I had a brainstorm while on the road, and I tapped the plastic sliding separator and asked the cabby to make a brief first stop at the Chemical Bank on the corner of Grove. The suggestion did not thrill him. I finally bought his cooperation with my last twenty, and he waited while I hit on the money machine. There were only two people ahead of me, and as it developed, they were a unit, so I got right to it, inserting my bank card, punching in the code. If

I had any doubts of divine guidance, they toppled as the machine stuck out its green tongue ten times and gave me the maximum allowed, thus enabling me to arrive home with a $200 bonus for accomplishing my shopping.

I checked to be sure the envelope was still safe under the mattress, with Pan Am's share plus the hundred or so I'd thoughtfully conserved for incidentals.

I never stopped moving. I packed, and during that ordeal I was forced frequently to curl up in a tight ball on the floor in order to alleviate the bouts of stress. It was disappointing, considering the impressive girth of my luggage, how little the unyielding interior held. The black cavity was filled before I'd hardly begun! I selected my favorite coolest, sheerest cottons and a few silk party pants and tops. The shoe situation was as grim as a pistol held to my head. Under this pressure I made my desperate choices. I closed the steel-framed cover, fastened the brass locks, and at four o'clock, right on schedule, I entered the cubicle large as the facility in the back of a Greyhound bus and took a cool bath. I shampooed and blow-dried my hair and filled the vanity case with the few toiletries it could hold. At quarter to five I was in my new chartreuse panties and net appliquéd bra, the room so hot I was as wet as if I'd been in the tub. My blue linen shirtdress was ready and waiting on a hanger looped over the geisha screen, a pair of black sling-back pumps neatly aligned beneath it.

There was one good-bye call I couldn't avoid. I dialed Marshall Springer, longing to connect with his irritating machine, but this round I didn't win.

"Hello." I got a prompt response.

"Hello, Marshall, it's me."

"Bad timing, Hope. No can talk."

"Marshall, I don't have time to talk either. I'll make it fast. So long, handsome, I'll drop you a line from Ustan."

Silence. "You'll what?"

"I'm in a hurry, Marshall. I have a ticket to be claimed and a plane to catch. I'm leaving in fifteen minutes, and ten of them are accounted for." I looked up at my shirtdress. It was quite unlike any garment I'd ever called my own. It didn't exactly scream *me*.

"Are you making this bullshit up?" he bellowed at me.

"It's not bullshit. What does the price of a ticket mean to Babi? Why shouldn't he send for me?"

"Send for you! What are you, a mail-order package?"

"This conversation I don't need."

I pulled the receiver away from my ear and got a voice-over, yelling, "Wait there! I'll be right over."

"There's no time. I still haven't hired a cab to take me to Kennedy."

"I'll drive you. Wait there."

"You'd really drive me?"

"Hope, you are driving me insane!"

"Marshall, since you're coming over, could you spare a few Valiums? Just a couple of hundred." I laughed like a maniac and hung up.

I got into my linen traveling costume, and with a black leather cummerbund giving it some shape, and the sling-backs supplying a touch of pizzazz, plus a black-and-white silk scarf tied at the open neck, the final effect wasn't too bad.

I paced back and forth, back and forth, maddened by the silence of the haunted house. I wasn't going to give Marshall more than the stipulated fifteen minutes, and he got in under the wire. He was panting like a horse, there was water dripping from his broad cheeks into his mustache, and his bib overalls were drenched. He took out a crumpled handkerchief and wiped his face and his hands.

"What the hell are you done up for? A Mary Tyler Moore look-alike contest?" He lowered his bushy eyebrows and glowered at me.

"You don't like it! It's not me!" My heart began to pound with anxiety.

"What's the story, Hope? What is this craziness you've concocted?"

"Let's talk while we drive. Marshall, I must pick up the ticket no later than seven. This is rush hour, let's go!"

"This is Sunday, dummy. This is New York. I'm Marshall, you're Hope, this is Grove Street. What the fuck is going on?"

I cringed from him. "Babi wired me a ticket. Why does that incense you so? I'm not an illegal alien. I'm allowed to leave this stinking country if I so wish."

"How dare that little runt send for you! Why doesn't he send for his wife? And you," he fired at me, "you can't give yourself twenty-four hours to reflect on it."

"He wants to see me. I want to see him. We want to see each other." I was shaking.

"Here." He tossed me a vial of Valiums. "If you're leaving, I won't be needing them any more."

I dropped them into my big black shoulder-strap bag but fast!

"This is truly the most unattractive move I have yet to see you make, to run the second this married man crooks a finger at you!"

"Since when did it become such an enormity to you that Babi is married? Leo is married, too, but you were always throwing me at his head!"

"Leo is different."

"Why is he different? Because he fought in some stinking six-day Jewish war?" I was bouncing my suitcase across the floor. Marshall didn't make a move to assist me.

"Leo is just a normal guy with faults, but Babi is your goddamn swamp!" He pushed me aside and seized the case by the thick leather handle, hoisting it on his back with a loud groan.

"What the hell do you have packed in here, Joanne's body? Where is Joanne? Where is Libby? Do they know you're leaving? Why aren't they here, seeing you off? I don't like this, Hope."

"I'm not uttering another syllable till I'm in a moving vehicle." I marched through the open door. My phone rang. I opened the outer door. My phone rang again.

"Your phone is ringing," Marshall said from behind.

"I know it's ringing. I'm not deaf." I was pretty sure it was Leo.

"Aren't you going to answer?"

I backtracked out of the rain. It was really pouring. "I know who it is."

"And you don't answer the phone unless it's a big surprise?"

To hell with the weather. I forged on, splashing through puddles to his familiar banged-up green panel truck. He heaved my cases into the rear. He climbed into the driver's seat and opened the broken right-hand door. I hopped up on the high running board and seated myself on the plain wooden kitchen chair held in place by ropes, thoughtfully reserved for the passenger. He started the windshield wipers. Only one of the wipers worked. His. I swear Marie Antoinette got delivered to the guillotine in a classier conveyance.

Marshall is a stone-silent driver. His concentration on the psychotic dawdlers blocking his progress is total. I whimpered a bit and let out an involuntary scream or two and asked if he was trying to kill both of us. In between screams and whimpers I told him about Joanne's accident, I told him about Libby's getaway to the Cape, I touched on the impending lawsuit. He had to agree, I appealed to his stony profile, that the ticket had come with marvelous timing. Why shouldn't I broaden my horizons, take a vacation, be good to myself for a change?

He double-parked at the entrance to the Pan Am Terminal. "I'll drop you here," he said. All of his attention was straight ahead.

"My bags, please," I timorously reminded him. The rain had subsided into a misty, foggy drizzle. Zero visibility.

Marshall lugged my bags as far as the porter at the door and left them there. He turned on his heels and made a run for his car.

"Aren't you going to wish me anything?" I caught his arm. I couldn't leave without Marshall's blessing.

He shook free and put his big hand on my shoulder. "Don't get sucked under, toots," was his fond farewell.

9

The less said about my Ustanian flight, the better Pan Am will like it. The jumbo jet touched down in Frankfurt, a detour no one had bothered to mention, and we were there for four miserable hours. I killed time in the duty-free store and ended up buying two bottles of Rémy Martin and the five allowed cartons of Vantage cigarettes. I got back into my seat in the middle of the middle aisle. I'd been informed, en route, that this weekly flight circled the globe. This information was imparted to me by the lecherous jeweler from Smyrna on my left, who was so protective and considerate of me he started to cut my inedible dinner meat. The delightful flight companion on my right was a mummy, rigid with fear, who radiated such an aura of terror I was forced to conclude it didn't feel so good to be dead. We were arriving at Hetron Airport five hours later than scheduled. That's what was troubling me, imagining the prince having to endure a five-hour wait, which might be more intense than the resigned nonwaiting of the past five years. I'd have thrown a tantrum if not for the stupefying combination of wine and Valium.

The scenes, the vibes at Hetron Airport are beyond description. These were a people who did not leave the blessed ground with confidence. If the shrieking and the hugging and the praying and the fainting I witnessed are what is commonly described as fatalism, I'd say it's just as well not to seek its comforts.

After baggage and customs and passport check and all that, my fellow survivors and I were released into a stadium-sized Quonset hut, and the din rising out of the assembly filling the vast space was louder than the roar of a charging brigade. I quivered against a cement wall. Posted along the perimeter of the enclosed stadium were men in turbans and skullcaps and head veils, wearing rumpled suits or sweeping robes, or shirts and huge pantaloons, and they were holding up sticks bearing placards inscribed with illegible squiggles, waving the placards around like protesters on a violent picket line. Had I walked into the middle of a spontaneous uprising or a junta? But then, wouldn't Babi be there, numbered among their leaders? Though I studied narrow, dark-eyed, bearded faces not unlike what could be Babi's, and my heart leaped in recognition a few false times, I did not find him. The chaos began to subside, the volume turned down, the stadium was emptying as gang after gang exited with its ecstatically claimed jet-setter, and no gang came forth to claim me.

What is the appropriate response to being stranded in the middle of the night in the middle of nowhere with a useless slab of tongue? I wholesomely gave vent to a rare attack of hysteria. Hope Diamond is never long ignored. Within moments a fascinated claque had gathered. We didn't achieve communication in at least a dozen incomprehensible languages.

A man crouched beside me as I clung to my case and stuck his face in mine. "Are you an American?" he asked in an irresistible Jimmy Stewart American accent. What bliss to plug back into the universe.

"God, yes!" A lifetime of love of country erupted from me.

"What's your problem?" He helped me to my feet. Jimmy was in a pilot's uniform. "Weren't you a passenger on flight two?"

"Yes!"

"Yeah, I noticed you in Frankfurt."

"Did you?" I gurgled, and bestowed a smile on my rapt audience, none of whom had taken so much as a step back.

"Mark, the limo is waiting," broadcast a female voice, and though the voice was undeniably American, my patriotism was not stirred.

"We have an American girl here in trouble. Can you get through this pack, Elaine?" He took charge and got the wall of onlookers to break it up.

"And what's her problem?" Elaine's blue eyes glazed indifferently over me. I was surprised she didn't take more of an interest in me, as we were equally fetching in our button-down navy blues, her stewardess uniform infinitely less wrinkled and rumpled than mine.

Mark looked to me to disclose my problem.

"My fiancé isn't here because you made the plane five hours later!" I decided to put the blame where it belonged.

"I don't really see the connection," Elaine answered in a lazy mountain twang. "Is your fiancé stationed here? Is he connected to our embassy or one of the American companies?"

"No," I said, and left it at that.

"Too bad, that would simplify matters. Well, he's probably on his way. Come on, Mark, I've got a six a.m. call." And she moved off, pulling her bag on a neat set of wheels and pulling Mark with her for good measure.

"Don't leave me here," I pleaded, and to Elaine's dismay, he didn't.

"Come on," he said, "and don't forget your gear." Fat chance.

Of course, my spirits lifted dramatically in the air-conditioned limousine taking the three of us to the Inter-Continental Hotel. Elaine, at the opposite window, warned me it might be completely booked. Really, I saw no indication of a thriving tourist trade.

"Where did you say your fiancé was stationed?" She startled me out of a fleeting reverie.

"Ray," I again told her. "It's a village on the Caspian Sea."

"The Caspian? You're lucky. That's the choice spot in this entire creepy place."

"Easy, Elaine." Captain Mark issued a warning. I suppose I could have been a spy. "What time do you have?" He angled his torso toward her.

Elaine checked her wristwatch. "Damn! I forgot to reset it in Frankfurt. What's the time difference from Ustan?"

"They're nine hours ahead of us," he told her, fiddling with his own watch.

"No. It's only eight hours from New York. What's the difference in Frankfurt time? We took off from there at eight-ten, wasn't it? Daylight saving time?"

They pooled their brains.

"Germany is six hours ahead during daylight, right, so it was two-ten, New York time."

"No, I'm sure it's only five hours." They gazed privately into each other's eyes. "If we're two hours ahead of Germany, and we set down in Frankfurt at approximately seven-ten, then it was about midnight, New York time."

"But departure from Frankfurt was delayed till eleven-fifteen."

"Their time?"

"No, our time. Oh, excuse me, of course, their time."

"No, Mark, you're getting it all screwed up. It was eleven-ten our time."

"But, Elaine, that's impossible. We left New York at eleven-fifty."

This debate went back and forth.

We were driving on a wide, smooth double highway separated by a center island planted every yard or so with high royal palms. There was a sliver of moon left, and stars, fading into an approaching dawn. Figures huddled around charcoal fires in the spaces between the trees. The highway narrowed into a single lane to pass through an archway in the base of a pyramid-shaped monument that suddenly loomed ahead. We had entered the capital city, and at its very beginning was the hotel, a square block of glass, its curved driveway and lobby lit up as if every night were a grand opening. The sky, streaked with rose and lilac, silhouetted a close horizon of flat-roofed structures and breast-shaped nippled domes and aerial-thin twin towers. Behind that man-made landscape loomed another silhouette of mountains with snaggled peaks that blotted out the sky.

I stepped out of the limousine into the heavy scent of flowers, and smiling gremlins in pointy-toed slippers fought over my bags as I floated into the deep freeze of the Inter-Continental lobby. The captain and his lady slipped off to their bridal suite and left me to face the bleary-eyed night clerk.

I posed a problem for the lone authority on duty—an unexpected American woman stepping out of a chauffeur-driven car at three in the morning with luggage that could have sunk the *Titanic,* and no wire, no warning, no reservation. The hotel was full. There was nothing available, nothing, nothing, nothing—he kept repeating the word as if it would make me vanish in a puff of smoke. All they had—and it was against all rules— was one empty and ready room being held for a 7:00 a.m. arrival. It would be necessary to evict me at 6:00 to give the maid an hour to prepare the room. I swore I wouldn't sleep on the sheets. As we stayed deadlocked in each other's hair-tearing dilemma, a possibility occurred to me that seemed increasingly likely upon instant replay.

"Could you tell me who is coming into the room tomorrow at seven a.m.?"

The night clerk went all cagey and suspicious. I must have been projecting intense spy vibrations. "Why do you ask, Miss Diamond?" We had gone through the necessary introductions. He, in fact, was holding my passport.

"I just thought it could possibly be my fiancé. You see, he was supposed to meet me at the airport, but maybe I got confused about dates. You don't happen to know for sure when Bastille Day falls, do you?"

An expression of tormented incomprehension made his whole face drop, every single fleshy feature drooping.

"May I ask you the name of your fiancé?" he said as his face slowly returned to its burdened—I could even say hostile—endurance of my stubborn presence.

I recited Babi's entire royal moniker, and his mobile features—the night clerk was a born character actor—rearranged themselves into an expression I can only describe as besotted.

"You are referring to our emir's nephew Prince Bahram?" Had any man ever regarded me with such ardor?

Though this exchange succeeded in bringing us closer and deepening our acquaintance, as fate would have it, the room was committed to a German engineer. It was mine, with no more questions, till 6:00 a.m. He could do no more for me. It could jeopardize his job. Would I explain his predicament to Prince Bahram?

"Will the prince be coming here to fetch you, Miss Diamond?"

"That is certainly what I anticipate," I answered, my thoughts translated from a strange language inexplicably available to me.

The clerk pressed a bell on the marble ledge between us, and those dancing gremlins sprang out from behind every marble pillar. I was escorted by the night clerk himself to the elevator, and he insisted on carrying my leather shoulder-strap bag and my customs shopping bag loaded with cigarettes and cognac. I was so numbed with fatigue I just blacked out on a flowered bedspread, which was the last thing I saw.

Six a.m. came like a hammerblow to the skull. Blindingly bright spots ignited in my head. The maid, an ageless woman in a long-sleeved cotton smock hanging over black cotton harem pants, every strand of her hair tucked into a snugly bound head scarf, must have been shaking me for quite a while. She conveyed her anxious timidity to be so disturbing a guest. She made helpless circular gestures with her open, empty hands.

I shimmied to the edge of the bed and hung there for a few crucial seconds, trying to remember where I was, who I was, and, not least important, if I was. Pain confirmed my existence. Every muscle of my body ached. Compelled to make the bed, the maid put her strong arms under my aching armpits and lifted me to an upright position. I chanced it and opened my eyes again. A wave of yellow nausea brought on a gagging reflex. My silent and frightened attendant quickly filled a glass from the bedside thermos. I drained it of every drop of ice-cold water and held it out for more. I could have remained there forever, drinking down sweet drafts of chilled water handed to me by this voiceless angel. It was somewhat reassuring to discover the yellow panic was not entirely of my own invention. What a yellowness saturated every inch of my borrowed room! The walls were yellow; the Formica-topped writing desk was yellow; the Naugahyde chair cushion was yellow; the drapes and matching bedspread were a flowered clash of yellows.

With the second glass downed, I entered the cruel joke of a yellow-tiled bathroom. The corpse in the mirror had died of jaundice. My navy blue slept-in pure linen traveling costume took on the green tinge of rotting vegetation. I was having myself one of those enviable moments of total self-realization it is my natural inclination to avoid. I pulled off my clothes and stepped into the uncurtained yellow-tiled shower stall. The water beating on me was the very essence of ecstasy, and I could have stayed there forever, but by then I'd remembered my mission and my prince and my growing suspicion that the giddy cable had misfired. I shampooed my hair with their shampoo, and there was even a blow dryer on the vanity, already plugged in.

When I emerged from my restoring ablutions, the angel was still in the room, and she had foolishly stripped the immaculate unslept-in sheets and was remaking the bed. The flowered drapes were pulled open, and it was nice to know the German engineer had a terrace outside his sliding glass doors that looked down on the hotel gardens and an Olympic-sized swimming pool, filled with water so blue and clear I could see straight down to the gigantic mermaid decorating the tile bottom.

Misfortune came fast on the heels of this cheerful interlude. No matter how many times I emptied the contents of my leather shoulder-strap bag on the yellow shag rug, no little envelope containing suitcase keys could be found. I struggled with the brass closures till my fingertips were red and raw as hamburger meat, but whatever falsities had passed the lips of the tormentor who sold me the monstrosity, she had not lied when she promised that nothing but the uniquely shaped key could open the damned thing. Had I left the keys at customs?

The maid had finished with the bed and was now vacuuming all around me, the whirring machine blocking any possibility of productive thought. I gave up the struggle. I went back to the bathroom and picked up the linen shirtdress off the damp mat. Still swathed in my yellow Turkish towel, I held out the atrocity, and when that didn't produce an instant response, I performed a full mute show of ironing the dress with my clenched fist. She finally got it, and after much negative head shaking and my plunking my behind on the Naugahyde desk chair, she scurried off to consult with her superiors. Be assured, I did not vacate the room until a steamed and pressed dress was mine to don. It had never been my plan to shock the prince into submission—if I ever *had* a plan.

It was surprisingly active and bustling downstairs at the ungodly hour of seven. Breakfast was being served in an American-style coffee shop that was only one of the many places to visit in the carpeted acreage of the immense lobby. Before anything else, I had a glass of fresh orange juice, a few cups of excellent American coffee, and a tiny nibble of buttered toast, and to my embarrassed horror, the eleven-dollar total on the bill was not an error. Yes, they did mean dollars, not whatever peculiar currency was native to Ustan.

A hotel official spotted me as I exited from that thieves' den and in excellent English begged me to accompany him to the desk. The friendly night clerk was gone, replaced by a crew who knew nothing and cared less about princes. They had no qualms about charging me for a full day's occupancy of the German's room, and my four hours of residence computed out to twenty-five dollars per. They returned my passport while making it expressively clear that no amount of money could buy me another hour's space in the fully booked hotel.

I decided to proceed to the village of Ray. I asked the manager, as a fully paid-up guest, how best to reach my final destination. From his startled reaction, I thought for a stomach-churning moment I'd come to the wrong country. The manager told me, and a few of the other hotel employees contributed to the discussion, that a weekly bus, departed the previous day, was the sole means of transport. I screamed. They offered, at no charge, to call the American Embassy, which might possibly help me locate my elusive fiancé. I said I'd rather walk the rest of the way. My proud independence provoked a round of merriment. Did I know what it entailed to cross the Elburz Mountains, which divided the capital city of Hetron from the Caspian? No one, with the exception of a tribe of fierce nomads who annually traversed the perilous range, could attempt such a feat. How could I doubt their sincerity and concern for my predicament? I didn't. Desolation gathered me to her bosom. Was it conceivable I should come so far and get no farther? I thanked them all for being so helpful and wondered if I might sit for a while on one of the lobby's multitudinous divans and reflect on my options. It was their pleasure.

I didn't reflect. I couldn't reflect. I just sat there in the opera house of a lobby, hung with giant chandeliers plunging down from a ceiling three stories high, a United Nations of a lobby, a hum of foreign voices, strange languages droning around me. And now, miracle of miracles, a voice was addressing me, in English, of all convenient coincidences.

"Miss Diamond?" It was the Inter-Continental manager, heroically managing to find the sight of me a suave delight.

"I'm afraid that's still my name," I archly replied.

"I believe we may have found a way for you to continue your journey to the village of Ray."

I clasped my hands to my chest.

"One of the young assistants at the desk took the liberty of speaking to one of our drivers, who are also on staff for the convenience of the Inter-Continental guests." He was talking really slowly in the English he'd learned to speak with an American accent. "It develops that this driver, who is the brother-in-law of our apprentice clerk, is from a village not a far distance from the village of your fiancé. He has business to attend to in his mother's house, and he would be glad to take you with him for a reasonable consideration."

"He'd go there today?" I stared up at the manager, who hung on my every word.

"That could be arranged."

"Arranged?"

"I could be persuaded to permit it." His liquid brown eyes spilled into mine.

I did some fast reckoning in my head. The cigarettes and booze had come to fifty. "I only have one hundred dollars with me."

"It is a very, very long and dangerous drive," he came back at me.

"Gosh, I just remembered," I said without snapping my fingers, "I do have another thirty dollars I completely overlooked." I was definitely hanging on to the last twenty.

"If you'll wait here, Miss Diamond, I will consult with the brother-in-law of my driver." He was not happy.

I waited as told while a horde of hotel employees converted my corner of the lobby into a restaurant, busily carrying out tables and straight-backed chairs, setting them before other divans similar to the one I'd appropriated. They unfurled snow-white tablecloths and laid heavy folded napkins, silverware, cut flowers in crystal vases. The international set began to drift in for lunch. The manager reappeared. The deal was on!

It was imperative that we set out immediately in order to cross the mountains before dark. Now that the mercenary part of the relationship was behind us, the manager and I remembered how much we liked each other. He wished me luck and declaimed how gratified the rest of his life would be in the knowledge that he had contributed to my reuniting with my fiancé. He ushered me to the revolving glass doors. The driver, Ali by name, thin and dark and young, was behind the wheel of a blue Volkswagen Rabbit, my bags piled neatly on the seat beside him. I let myself into the back seat, and we were on our way. Allah is the greatest!

Allah got us to the very end of the driveway, where we merged with the midday traffic and proceeded to be boiled alive for the two hours it took to cover approximately ten city

blocks. We were hemmed in by a crunch of automobiles crawling in and out and around each other, banging fenders and
bumpers, like blind lobsters desperately groping to escape the
searing basin and instinctively climbing up onto the mountainside. Whatever fellow figured out hell was a hot place was
no stranger to Hetron traffic.

We moved faster as we began the gentle rise into the mountains. There were high walls on either side of the broad avenue,
and behind the walls I caught green flashes of gardens and big
houses. As the avenue narrowed into a road and the rise got
steeper and stonier, the landscape turned brown and barren, the
walls ceased to be, and on either side of us were square earthen
shacks; and along the edges of the winding road an occasional
veiled woman walked behind a thin, turbaned peasant leading a
slow-moving mule. The vista was positively biblical.

Ali and I were linguistically incapable of enjoying the workings of each other's minds, but he seemed sufficiently entertained by a rock and roll station blasting out of the car radio,
and I was more than entertained by staring down into the
abyss, sheer drops that turned my knees to jelly. It was lunacy
that any race of mortals had decided these mountains were put
there to be crossed, which they surely were not, at least not by
civilized people. I wasn't aware of when our descent began, but
begin it did. On the downward side the mountains began to be
spotted with green foliage; then the green thickened, and trees
and brush of every possible tint of green blanketed and concealed every inch of the brown earth. The sky started to
darken—at least it became less brilliantly white—and Ali pulled
the car to a perilous stop on the shelf we were negotiating, removed a small rug from under the driver's seat, and there and
then performed a series of prostrations.

It was dark when the wheels of the car were rolling on level
land. Ali pulled into a front yard and turned off the motor.
There was a house a few feet back with a platform built onto

the front. Veiled women stooped over smoking headhunter pots, dogs howled, and I shivered in the cool night. If I knew nothing else, I knew this was not the palace of the prince.

Ali opened his door and then mine, and I followed him on stiff pins-and-needles legs. These people may have been his family, as there was a great deal of embracing and bowing. A group of skullcapped men sat to one side of the platform, rugs beneath them, playing a game with clicking dice. A woman with a babushka took me through a windowless room to a backyard where I might answer the pressing call of nature. She stood at a discreet distance and silently returned me to the party up front. Children and women gathered around, touching my linen dress, giving my shoulder-strap bag a feel. One child pinched my bare legs. He's selling me to these barbarians, I thought for one swooning moment. I was offered a bowl of food and a glass of hot tea, and though I couldn't swallow the native fare, the tea was ambrosia.

We killed a good hour there, me jumping out of my skin. Finally Ali commenced the ceremonious good-byes, and we took off. We drove till it seemed to me the drive had no destination, it was simply itself, when Ali finally slowed down, stopped, and turned off the engine but not the headlights. They beamed on a flight of stone steps hacked out of the side of the mountain at the end of the earth. The only sound I could hear was my own blood whooshing in my ears. Ali got my bags out and started up the stone steps, motioning to me to follow. As if wild horses could force me to stay behind! The steps were a winding ribbon ending at a thick, looming wall. Set in the wall were high portals and a hanging bell that Ali rang, setting off a chain of ringing bouncing back at us from all sides. Voices sprang to life on the other side of the wall. My heart was in my mouth. Would I see my Babi now? Would the prince throw open his mighty gates to me?

A peasant dressed in funny pajamas, a skullcap on his head,

stepped through the opening of a smaller door cut inside the heavy portals. A veiled woman fleet as a goblin joined him. They both held lanterns lifted high to enable them to see us. Ali and the pajamaed peasant spoke back and forth, back and forth; the goblin had a tongue in her head, too. They all shrugged and looked at me, and the couple pointed up at the mountain and down at the mountain—what confusion! But Ali must have convinced them to accept the delivery.

I followed the flowing veils through a room with a high, vaulted ceiling, and then another pitch-black room, then through an archway, and ahead of me was a wall-enclosed courtyard, stars in the skies, shadows of trees. I followed the goblin along an outside passageway that traveled along the side of a low barracks of a building, with closed doors every ten or twenty steps. I thought—if I was thinking—we must be in the servants' quarters.

She opened the last door of the row of doors and motioned to me to enter. I stepped over a ledge into a square cell of a room. She placed her lantern on the floor beside a low cot fitted with a thin cloth mattress. Her husband came in after us, carting my bags. He dropped them to the floor and quickly stepped out, waiting for her at the open door. She uttered a few incomprehensible but kind-sounding words to me and, leaving the lantern behind, backed out and closed the door, sealing me into the isolated cell. It was not the welcome I would have envisioned, if I trafficked in visions. I lowered myself to the thin mattress, my head finding a stiff, cylindrical pillow, and from that reclining position I could look through a grilled window set directly under the low beamed ceiling. It was a comfort to see the distant glow of a charcoal fire.

10

My eyes weren't closed for more than a second when someone was beaming a flashlight directly on the lids, forcing them open and singeing my eyeballs with a blaze of sunlight. I blinked and huddled against the rough wall, squinting into the sunshine to identify a figure seated on the floor beside my cot.

"Babi?" I timidly ventured. I couldn't hear myself speak. The din of hammering and drilling and strange guttural calls invaded the cubicle. Were marauders tunneling their way through the tiled floor? "What is that?" I said, half warning the motionless man.

"It's nothing. It's only the workers repairing the underground vaults. Ignore them, Hope. We have more pressing matters to discuss. Why have you come here?"

It was his sultry voice, his black eyes behind steel-rimmed glasses watching me. It was Babi's slight body buttoned into a long white robe, his large head, his clipped black beard, his narrow and sensuous visage. My darling. I covered the ruined face I'd been traveling in for too many days.

"Look at me, Hope!" he ordered, and I did as I was told. It hurt to look at him. The brilliant stream of sun pouring through the open doorway blurred him in a ball of iridescent light. The noise and the light numbed my senses. "Why are you here?" he said.

"Babi, I had to find you."

"Find me? I was unaware of the fact I was missing. In my simple mind, I considered my absent wife to be the missing person."

He was angry. I hadn't prepared myself for anger. I was ready, I guess, for him to be stunned, but then so glad of the surprise.

"One day I come home to find my wife gone," he continued in his deadly tone, "and this morning I am alerted by the servants that another foreign lady has arrived in her place. My servants are not accustomed to delivering amusing announcements to me on the comings and goings of my household." His accent, thicker than it used to be, in no way prevented the voluble flow of words.

I clutched my head, as much to block his words as the incessant hammering outside the grilled window.

"Did my wife accompany you to Ustan, Hope? Has she waited behind in Hetron?"

Again Joanne. The only discord that had ever reared its ugly head between us.

"No, I came alone. Babi," I said, "I was so worried about you I was frantic. I wrote to you. I even cabled you."

"Cables, here." He snorted at the absurdity of the notion.

"You should have answered my letters if you didn't want me to come. I thought you needed me. . . ."

"I did answer, over a week ago. Answering correspondence is not my only duty, Hope."

"Joanne kept telling me you were off on a pilgrimage. It didn't seem possible."

"I have been on a pilgrimage till recently." He paused. "How is my wife adjusting to America?"

Why did he keep calling her that? I knew her name.

"She's all right." An image of a bandaged, bobbing head flitted across my mental screen. "She's moved in with her mother. Libby's house is falling down. I had nowhere to go, Babi."

He silently regarded me and then clapped his palms together in a few resounding slaps. As if she'd been waiting for his signal, a servant, dressed not unlike the Inter-Continental maid, slipped in. He spoke to her in their make-believe language, and she vanished as noiselessly as she appeared.

"Fatima will bring us tea," he told me, and then he sighed.

"Hope, it pains me deeply to receive you in my house in so harsh a manner. Who is closer to my heart or more precious to me than you, my dear good friend? But to arrive this way, with no warning—it is so awkward for me. You had only to express a wish to visit and I would have arranged it all, properly, in its proper time."

The banging and thumping still shaking my insides began to subside, and soon there was silence. Fatima returned, carrying a round bronze tray that held two water glasses of steaming tea. She set the tray on the rug beside her master, and a jolt of panic all but tossed me to the floor. It was Libby's rug the prince sat upon, the rug I'd sold to Hossein. Across the room was a mirrored wardrobe, and for one crazy moment I thought they'd both come dancing out from behind it, accusing me of my crime. Fatima closed the door on us, and the dimness and the silence embraced me as the prince had not. I sipped the hot sweet tea, and the sweetness soaked into my tongue before it reached my throat.

"Are you telling me the truth, Hope? You've come this immense distance all alone, provoked only by an overpowering desire to see me?"

I stared at him. Only?

"There is something else brewing." He studied me as if my face might give him a clue. "If it's about my wife, don't be afraid of hurting me by speaking out now, immediately. I know the woman was holding back some information from me or she wouldn't have left in that ridiculous fashion. Why should she wish to create a scandal? If she needed to go home, even permanently, she had but to tell me and all would have been properly and discreetly arranged." I saw him remember having just said those exact words. "Why must you arrive this way, not eagerly anticipated, but thrust upon me, not letting me have any say? Hope, Hope," he groaned, and pressed his fingers into his temples, "listen to how I am speaking to you. I am ashamed of my own words to you, the woman who took me into her heart and country so tenderly, so protectively, and who witnessed my foolish fight against the forces of ignorance, when I became as ignorant as my adversary. Hope, please forgive me. It's only my silly dislike of the erratic, the thoughtless—and yet that is part of life, too." He rocked pensively, his expression pained.

"Babi, I didn't come here to hurt you. I won't be erratic and upset your household. And I wasn't being thoughtless—it was something else. I needed to come to you, Babi. I had to get out of there."

"Has New York become that bad?" He said this in a normal, curious tone. "I hear terrible things about the decay of the whole city. I'm always so sorry to hear it. I really dug New York. Those were mad years, but I am so thankful to have had them. However, they have no place in my life now." He stood up and gazed down at me, his expression a mixture of tenderness and threat.

"Babi, this is Hope you're talking to." I pressed my hand flat on my heart. "No one was more opposed to the madness than I. What have I ever wanted but some sense of order? I needed a place, Babi, where I could stop turning in circles. I needed to think. I needed some peace. There comes a time when you need to rest."

He put his hand on my head. "Hope, you are welcome in my house. I am truly touched and flattered that you would come to me for this solace from American insanity. You are welcome to stay, Hope, as long as it pleases you." And then he took a deep breath, as if a great burden had fallen from his shoulders, and his face got three shades lighter. "I must leave you now," he told me. "My uncle Karim has come today to discuss family business. You will meet him at lunch. In the meanwhile," he continued in a conversational tone, "my young cousin Yasmin, who has been for the past three years in England learning

English, is staying at the palace to protect my motherless son from the indulgences of the servants." He put on a dizzy face to suggest the heady degrees of those indulgences. "Yasmin is an orphan, poor girl, who has long been the ward, and almost as close as a daughter, to my elder sister, Nassrim. She is very sweet-tempered and kindhearted, and I am sure you will be tolerant of her limitations." He stroked his close-cropped black beard as if it were a pampered pet.

"That's my specialty, tolerating limitations." I laughed with relief to be in his confidence again.

"It's good to hear your laugh, Hope. Never have I laughed the way I laughed with you." He sounded as though he were in mourning for laughter.

"We were a happy couple, weren't we, Babi?"

The prince tensed, and his shoulders inside the long white robe lifted in a defensive gesture. "There is something I might mention. . . ." He was having trouble continuing.

"What is it, Babi? Say it. You can say anything you want to say to me."

"The legal fact of our marriage—my family is ignorant of it. And your presence here, in my house, might confuse them." His accent had thickened with the effort of forcing his thoughts out in English.

"Marriage," I chided him. "Was that a marriage we had, or was it a courtship, a constant courtship?"

I stood up, and there we were, face-to-face, the same perfect height. He took my head between his two long-fingered hands and lightly kissed my forehead, and my nose, and my lips.

"Thank you for your understanding, Hope," he said, and was gone.

Fatima came in and led me to the adjoining facilities. I accepted by then that my blue linen dress was permanently grafted to my skin. The walled courtyard outside the cell I'd dozed in was alive with activity. Servants were hanging sheets on lines strung up between high, narrow trees. A gardener was busy watering flowering bushes a safe distance from them, and in the middle of it all a kid, hardly more than a baby, was kicking up water and making a lot of noise in a plastic wading pool, a four-posted awning protectively shading the spot. The sun was really strong. Anywhere it touched, you felt it, hot and heavy. The dark bathroom, with only a slit in the tiled walls to let in light, was as humble in its austere way as my chamber. The fixtures were all white and functional and had the feeling of being recently installed. I couldn't find anything that resembled a switch to turn on a light, and there wasn't even a mirror not to see anything in. Was it possible these servants' quarters had no electricity? Was it possible the entire palace had no electricity? I washed my face and dried it on a dish towel that seemed to be there for that purpose. There was no point in showering. The first order of business was to unpack the valise, break the damn thing open.

The child who'd been splashing in the wading pool was in my room, wading through the contents of my shoulder-strap bag. He looked up at me, and it was Babi, before I ever knew him.

"Hello," I said, in the wonderful manner I have with children. "My name is Hope. What is your name?"

He got coy with me and returned to rifling through my things.

I knelt down next to him. "What are you looking for?" Joanne had proudly mentioned he could speak English, but by now it might all have been forgotten. He'd be relearning it with a very patient teacher.

"Present for Abbas?" the child said.

I could have kicked myself. "Yes," I said, "of course, Hope has a present for Abbas."

I dumped out the rest of the bag's contents, and what should be there, staring me in the face, but the envelope containing the specially shaped valise key. I thought I was seeing a mirage.

That gave me time. "Come here," I told him. "The present is in here." And I pointed at the genuine cowhide leather, steel-framed, brass-buckled, thirty-nine-inch gorilla lying unconscious in the middle of the floor.

Abbas crouched beside me, liking the game. His skin smelled sweet, and his tousled black curls grazed my knuckles as he intently followed the unlocking of the treasure chest. He was very tiny and delicate in his blue bathing bloomers.

A female voice behind us sang out an aria in the quaint local tongue, and Abbas, the bilingual, leaped up from his crouch beside me. The female's stream of words continued, and Abbas turned his back on the amusing hunt and streaked out of the room.

"I do hope my cousin's naughty boy has not been a bother to you." It was Yasmin, the poor girl I was expected to tolerate. She stood there in bare feet, long, bare, smooth legs, white short-shorts, a bare midriff, a turquoise puffed-sleeve top tied in a knot between her rounded bosoms, and a small, elegant head of black hair pulled back from her languid face and plaited in one thick braid hanging down her back. So this was what they'd kept hidden under the veil. "You will excuse my faulty English, please," she said, supposing that my stupefaction reflected a communications breakdown.

"Your English is excellent," I said.

"Oh, it is not." It had one dimple, too, and pink, moist lips, and an eagle's nose, and eyes the color of gold. "I am Yasmin." She supplied the unnecessary. "And you are the American friend Hope come to visit my cousin Prince Bahram?" It wasn't really a question. "It is my great pleasure to meet you," she said.

I smiled at her. It was difficult not to.

"You were going to unpack your dresses? May I help you?" Her eyes glinted with curiosity at the hidden wonders hunkering at our feet.

"I don't know if I should unpack. Is this my room?"

"If you do not like it, you can have another. You can have mine. It is like this; all the rooms in the women's quarters are like this one. It is the horror of these old palaces." She laughed and slid her eyes back to the fascination of the suitcase. "Shall I help you now with your dresses?"

Now was as good a time as any. The sooner I got out of the crushed linen, the less painful the amputation would be. I knelt at the jaws of the beast, twisted the key, and flung back its head. A few of its black guts spilled out. I removed the black fringed shawl on top and shook it out.

Yasmin released an involuntary gasp and jumped out of my way, her slender fingers with their pale, oval nails flying to her lips to hold back the next cry. "All black. So much black. Oh, Hope, your husband, he is dead?"

I stared down into the blackness. I said nothing.

"Hope, excuse me. I have made you sad." She had the courage to move in closer. "It is recent, this death?"

"My husband isn't dead!" I pulled out the black silk evening pajamas.

She shook her head and the thick braid didn't budge. "I am so stupid, Hope. In my country it is a respect for a widowed lady to wear black. But black can be very smart, very chic. I love black," she assured me. "I have loved very much the black gowns of Valentino. But my cousin Prince Bahram—he does not like the women to wear black."

I walked away from the dreaded valise. Would they serve me my meals in here? I pillaged the duty-free plastic shopping bag and fell on the cot, tearing open one of the Vantage cartons.

Yasmin came and sat beside me. "You have more dresses that will arrive tomorrow?" She lightly touched my arm. "I have been here two weeks, and I waited many days for my things to come from London, where I have been studying. And many of my cases have not yet arrived."

There were matches in the plastic bag. I lit up and inhaled

the toxic fumes, trying to turn one long drag into a successful suicide. My head rolled back against the wall, and I gazed out through the high window to admire the view. There was nothing to see but the mountainside and maybe an inch of sky. I could follow a string of a meandering footpath leading to a lone peculiar structure, a kind of deck. It looked so bleak and lonely I didn't envy the watchman who must have been up there last night, feeding his charcoal fire. On the blue-tiled floor below the window was a stack of pillows. The mirrored wardrobe completed the furnishings. It would not be a difficult cell to keep tidy.

"Hope," Yasmin was imploring me, "I could please have one of your American cigarettes?"

"You smoke?" I was astounded. I handed her the pack. "Here," I said, "keep it. It's a present."

"You are too kind. I can't accept, Hope." She dropped the pack between us. "The servants would report it to my cousin. They are all spies. And Prince Bahram would not like this information." She held a match to the tip of her cigarette and expertly sucked in smoke, her nostrils curling with pleasure. "Ahhh," she blissfully expelled a cloud of smoke. "Soon I am going to Paris with Nassrim," she told me, joyously filling her lungs with more smoke, "and there I will do anything I wish. Come." She jumped up and gripped my hands. "Come with me. I will find you the brightest, most beautiful dress to wear to please Prince Bahram. He is so sad, so serious, Hope—and not so old, only twelve years more than I."

She held onto my hand and led me to a room physically similar to mine, except this one had been converted into an overstocked boutique. There were rods running the length of the ceiling, hung with gowns and capes and robes; and there were sets of rods, one above the other, precisely, perfectly hung with rows of silk shirts and skirts and embroidered jackets and tweed jackets and silk jackets; and scarves and belts and ribbons filled hooks attached to the wall; and there were shelves with neatly folded sweaters and lingerie; and rows and rows of polished shoes. There were steamer trunks holding God knows what, and in the middle of it all, an oval full-length mirror, the kind that tilts inside a frame.

"These are my dresses, Hope," she introduced us. "Many of my aunts who arrive now on the Caspian have been bringing me dresses from Europe. You will let me find something I like, for you?" She was authentically excited at the prospect of dressing me, no doubt the biggest challenge she had attempted since dressing her last baby doll. "First, please to let me give you a more personal gift." She carefully draped a silvery white silk caftan trimmed with braided gold over my arms.

"Yasmin, are you sure? It isn't necessary. . . ." I stared down at the waterfall of silk. The fabric shimmered with waves woven into it.

"Oh, please, Hope, it is my gift. These others I will find for you, we will decide later." She was embarrassed at her covetousness, and her face flushed a glorious burnished gold. She hung her head.

"Yasmin, don't be silly. Come on." I tried to cheer her up, restore her high spirits. "You were going to make me a joy for the prince. And I am sure you will do an excellent job."

My coddling worked. Yasmin began a pirouette around her splendid achievement. She pulled up in front of me to fix me in a long professional gaze. Gone was the child—this was a technician at the controls.

"Do you know, Hope, you look very much like an Ustanian woman—your eyes, so pretty. Here is a tunic." She held it up in front of me and critically appraised the effect. "Yes," she congratulated herself, "I was right." It was an ecru-colored and embroidered sheer cotton top, folds falling into a floating column. "And this." She thrust a shirred skirt at me, blood-red and so sheer I could see the grime under my fingernails through the transparent cloth.

"I couldn't wear this," I laughed.

"The top is long enough to cover all. It is just for today, Hope. For me." Her concerned eyes tore off my navy blue penitential garb and traveled down to my bare feet. "Shoes," she whimpered, "shoes are the most difficult." Her crystal-clear eyes went cloudy with pain. "The shoes in Ustan . . ." Her whole being tensed to communicate the enormity of the subject. "Dresses, even lovely French dresses, one may find in the hotel shops of Hetron, but shoes . . ." Again the effort to convey the staggering implications.

"I'll manage," I said, trying to remember the black assortment buried inside the valise.

"Yasmin . . . Yasmin . . ." The air carried the sound of her name.

"I must attend to my duties." She flushed her sun-drenched color again. "Good-bye, Hope. I will come to fetch you at lunchtime." And she closed up shop.

I carried my new acquisitions into the dim and pleasantly cool cell. I finished unpacking. It was not a drawn-out production. I extracted the new undies and dug out my summer sandals, the flat ones and the high-heeled crippling ones. I promptly relocked the locks and stashed the remains between the mirrored wardrobe and the wall. I opened the square vanity case and got some good news. There was a mirror on the inside lid. I showered and shampooed my hair, blow dryer or no blow dryer, and combed the wet hair back for it to hang out and dry. I repaired my face and even applied an extra layer of kohl. The sheer cotton felt like wings tickling my skin, and it made me giddy to meet this brand-new creature from the deep lagoon in the streaked wardrobe mirror.

Yasmin made sure there was sufficient time for a leisurely cigarette before we set off for lunch in the front garden connected to the prince's private rooms. She oohed and ahhed over me, and shamelessly took all the credit for my newly revealed beauty. She was wearing a short white pleated tennis skirt and an off-the-shoulder diagonal red-and-white-striped snug-fitting jersey top and white stiletto-heeled sandals, a single strap across her high instep. She was as adorable as a kid playing dress-up—a sexy, sultry kid. And guileless—there seemed not to be a competitive cell in her precociously matured body.

"What pleasure you will give to Prince Bahram. I am so happy you have come to help me cheer my cousin's wifeless household." Smoke streamed joyously from her flaring nostrils. Her hair was piled in a loose knot that let a few silky strands fly free. I touched my own hair.

"I'd cheer him a lot more if I had the use of my hair dryer."

The language barrier was up. "I do not understand you, Hope."

"This," I explained, pulling the implement out of my vanity case. "It works on electricity." I mimed plugging the plug into space.

"But there is electricity in the palace. Prince Bahram has a very big machine to make electricity, near the kitchens." She waved her hand in a backward direction. "If you have a need or an emergency, he will be very glad to make the electricity work. Ask him, Hope."

I said I'd rather not.

I had a short tour of the palace on the way to lunch. The rooms were not especially spacious or high, and they came in a variety of sizes. Some of the floors I walked on were marble, and there were rugs everywhere, and tile halfway up walls that became as rough as the insides of an unfinished building. All was shadowed and shaded within, the windows more like portholes or vents, crisscrossed with iron gratings or sealed closed with multicolored bubbled glass. The space above the tile was hung with calligraphy, and I noticed a few portraits of elaborately uniformed toy soldiers from a remote past. I found myself in a wide marble hall, open at the far end, the floors uncarpeted; the marble floor extended into an outside terrace, and there, under the shade of a sharply angled awning, were the prince and his son and a few other guests, seated on cushions arranged around a low platform of a table. Relays of servants were using an outside path, coming from some unseen source with platters and tureens of food.

Yasmin promptly claimed the cushion next to an elderly gray-haired gentleman in white linen slacks and a dark green tricot shirt, a silk foulard at his throat.

"At last the most important reason for lunch arrives," the gentleman said without rising, but his greeting, in English learned from French, was graciously intended for the foreigner in their midst.

The cushion between the prince and his uncle appeared to be reserved for me.

"Hope, if you will permit me, I would present His Excellency my uncle Karim. I've told him how fortunate I feel to be able to return even the smallest part of your American kindness to me."

The revelation of my incredible kindness tipped the scales for Karim, and he fell on my hand with a direct hit to his heart. He lifted his head, crowned with a shock of slicked-back iron gray hair. His eyes were deep-set as an eagle's eyes, and his lips were still tasting the world.

"Your outfit is so charming. I wish more of our women appreciated the beauty of Ustan's graceful styles. But all they want to hear is Paris, Paris, Paris." He smiled at me, his strong teeth the color of aging ivory. He turned to Babi and spoke a long and amused statement in their exotic tongue. Then to me: "I was telling my nephew that I now understand why he is so angry to leave his home for even a few days." My expression of bafflement got through to Karim. "Our beloved emir"—the two men exchanged sly smiles—"has requested an immediate visit from your host."

"Oh, how wonderful! I long to see our emir's Caspian palace." It was Yasmin, speaking English over food that spoke another language.

The prince seemed wounded by Yasmin's elation. Without responding to her enthusiasm, he took up his plate and began heaping it with vast quantities of rice and ragouts and vegetable stews, pouring a white yogurt sauce over the huge portion of food. We all followed suit. Despite my previous prejudice regarding luncheons, I discovered I was hungry, too. Karim was my attentive guide to the culinary mysteries. He spoke knowledgeably of the assorted delicacies and highly recommended the kebabs and thought I might enjoy some simple rice, made only with herbs and walnuts, and knew where every lemon, every eggplant and tomato, every chunk of melon had been plucked.

I had never seen Babi eat with such dedication. He never lifted his face—except to acknowledge Abbas, who snuggled lovingly against his father, lifting his open mouth for choice tidbits like a fledgling bird—until his plate was wiped clean with strips of the delicious hot flatbreads. Lunch, as it developed, was not only the prince's main repast of his long day but it frequently was the only meal he attended. With the last morsel consumed, Babi lifted his napkin to his lips, set like a moist orchid inside the black foliage, and launched into a serious exchange with his uncle, both of them apologizing for speaking in a language unfamiliar to their guest.

Yasmin had become a child at the table, picking at her food, squabbling with Abbas, pouting, and addressing sharp words to one of the servants. "I am tired." She stood up abruptly, causing the men to pause in their rapid locution. She never for a second concealed her boredom.

"Go, Yasmin, dear." Karim kissed her forehead. "Enjoy your midday rest. You will find something I have brought you from Paris in your room." Well, that cheered the girl. She skipped into the house as Karim leveled his attention on me. "And you, Hope, are you tired, too?"

I looked to Babi to find out.

Karim chatted on in English. "I detest this practice of wasted afternoon hours. It is not so hot up here. Of course, in our deserts it is different. But I've lived so long in France I find the practice abominable. It is so much better to exercise after a heavy meal. To promenade, as they do in Paris. Could I coax you to walk in the garden with me?" His business with the prince was evidently concluded.

"You should go with my uncle Karim to the garden, Hope," the prince recommended. "The garden is unique, and no one knows its secrets better than Karim."

I wasn't dying for a walk. I would have preferred reclining there and charming Babi out of his melancholy mood. But I was being assisted to my feet.

"Oh, but she must have something for her head," Karim remembered. His request was tom-tommed through the tribe of servants, and one appeared, carrying a panama hat for him and a silk parasol intended for me.

"Enjoy your walk," Babi said, with a smile so familiar my heart leaped to receive it. It was as if the old Babi, my Babi, had peeked out from behind this guarded face.

Karim took me to a garden lying like an immense colored carpet at the foot of a mountain. I didn't realize it was the mountain visible from my high grated window till I recognized the wooden structure, suspended on the slope like a becalmed vessel. There was even a motionless sail shading the deck.

"I haven't seen this garden for a full year. My nephew has made some wonderful additions. Aren't these jonquils magnificent?" He moved ahead of me, holding onto my arm as though he were helping me out of a car. My thin-soled sandals were not treading the surface they had been whimsically designed for. Karim plunged up the slight incline in a great display of stamina and vigor. He exuded energy.

"Do you live in Paris most of the time?" I asked, slowing

him down, as I did not wish to convert this promenade into a physical fitness exercise.

"I divide my time between Paris and a few other places I am fond of." He plucked a white blossom off a bush and briskly scrubbed it between his palms. Then he sank his face into his cupped hands as if he were lapping up water. "Smell." He held his palm out to me. A musky, pungent odor filled my head.

"Ummmm," I appreciatively droned. "Lovely." I stumbled after him.

"Come out of the sun," he urged me, and pulled me under a shady tree that had a complicated-looking cushioned swing hanging from one of its high, fat branches. It actually turned out to be quite comfortable, and it was wide enough for us to sit together, so long as I crossed my legs and hung over my side, clinging to the thick silk cord it swung on.

"I know so little of you, Hope, only that you are a friend of my nephew from his American student days. Were you students together?"

"Practically," I said. The rocking of the swing clobbered me with jet lag.

"And you are a friend of his American wife, Joanne, as well?"

"More an acquaintance," I answered.

"I hardly know her at all, I am so little here. I was sorry to hear of their current upheaval. Are you married?" he quickly added.

"No," I said. His arm had curled around my waist.

"Have you never been married?"

"I was, once," I said, "but I'd rather not talk about it."

"Of course. Those matters are private. I, too, was married, happily, but my wife has been dead now for many years. She came back to Ustan at the end of her life, which, of course, I permitted, but I could not accompany her as I was still in exile. Aren't those poplars magnificent?" He pointed them out for me.

"Was that very difficult for you, to be exiled from your own country?"

"At first," he said, with an indifferent shrug, "but now I am free to come and go at will, and I have no wish to live here again. It is such a small, repetitious cycle of events, all of the nobles held in the shadow cast by our most brilliantly illuminated emir." His thorny eyebrows lifted, and his eyes checked to see if I'd got the message. "I prefer not to be so close to the light shed by our exalted ruler. But for a summer, here on the Caspian, it is very nice indeed. And to find so captivating a creature as you enjoying Prince Bahram's hospitality—that is a great stroke of luck. You are staying at least through the summer, I hope. I will be the guest of my niece Nassrim until the end of August."

"Will you?" I said, pressing a yawn back into my face.

"You haven't yet met Princess Nassrim, the prince's elder sister, have you? Surely you will come to her dinner party tonight. Her villa is on the sea, a five-mile drive from this old fortress, and these dinner parties, though mostly family, can be quite entertaining. Do you have a family in America, Hope?"

"No," I said.

"How sad, a woman without a family. In Ustan it would be perilous, but in America it is quite common. Do you live alone in New York?"

I put my head back. The sky was a white ceiling, resting on the walls of mountains. High as the castle was, the perch did not feel open, but hemmed in, all those mountains, all so dark and thick with a jungle of trees. Even the garden was close and dense around me.

"Excuse me, that is too personal a question." He misread my silence. "Have you ever been to Paris? You are familiar with the City of Lights?"

"Of course," I said.

"And you liked Paris?"

"Loved it." I was drifting off on the swing.

"Perhaps you might come one day and visit me there. I have an adequate set of rooms I keep at the Plaza-Athénée, though I must move soon—the hotel is becoming overrun with Arabs." His sharp old face broke into a grin. "But there is always my shack in Antibes to escape to, and my boat. I am a man of simple habits, simple tastes. Beautiful boats and beautiful women—those are my only extravagances. Come." He helped me off the swing. "I am tiring you. How selfish of me, after your long flight." His hard fingers slipped under my wide sheer sleeve and caressed the bare flesh of my arm. "You resemble one of our women," he told me as we started back. "Your parents, they are not of American descent, are they?"

"They're dead," I said.

"But before they died," he said with a chuckle, "and their parents before them—from where in Europe did they migrate to America?"

I could not elude the inquisitor. "Well, centuries ago my mother's family resided in Russia."

"Of course!" he said, as if I'd proved him right, verified his case. "We are very close as people. Ustan shares a border with Russia as well as the Caspian Sea."

"I'm so glad," I said.

"And your father, and his ancestry, it was also Russian?"

I was slipping into the numbing fatigue that produces false confessions. I had to rouse myself before my interrogator extracted all my secrets. "What are those purple flowers over there, Karim?" I slipped off the swing, my feet on terra firma. He had to scramble after me, shielding me with the raised parasol.

"Those are a breed of orchid indigenous to this Caspian coast," he meticulously informed me.

"I'd love one." I beamed at him, and two, then three were thrust upon me.

"I have a dear friend, a woman friend, in Paris," he remarked as we strolled along an avenue of poplars leading back to the palace. "Since my wife's death she has been my closest friend— a superb, intelligent female. She, too, has a mother of Russian descent, though Nicole herself is, of course, French, a French Jewess," he said, his eyes measuring me till they clicked like the shutter of a camera. He brushed my knuckles with soft, full lips and left me at the passage to the women's quarters.

Yasmin kept dashing in and out of my dark chamber, bearing gifts, hanging flowing favors on the hooks jutting out of my plain whitewashed walls. A paralysis thick as a spell kept me immobilized on my thin mat. It was completely dark when she came in, holding a lantern and dressed in a diaphanous chiffon robe.

"I see you are too tired to come with me and Karim to Nassrim's dinner party." She brushed back my hair. "Sleep tonight, Hope. My cousin Prince Bahram also will remain at the palace as he must prepare for his early departure to the emir's Caspian court. He will like the company of a woman in his house."

I lay alone in the dark room, wondering if I should freshen up for the prince's visit. If I closed my eyes and opened them again, would he be there at my feet, as he'd been this morning? I lay for a long time, gazing through the grated window till I sighted the comforting flare of the sentry's charcoal fire. I didn't realize I was crying until I touched my wet face. Why was I crying? Were these the fabled tears of joy? What if they effortlessly released themselves till my body was left a dry husk, so weightless it could lift from the cot and be carried, unresisting, to be extinguished in the glowing coals?

11

Morning brought Yasmin boogying into my dreams to the blasting strains of a cassette-radio, the toy given to her by Uncle Karim. She was radiant with excitement.

"Now we can dance!" she cried aloud over the booming music. "Do you like to dance, Hope? I love to dance. There must be so many new dances in America. You will teach them to me? In London I went sometimes to dance. Do they dance the pogo now in New York?" And she gyrated her hips and swayed on her long legs, naked to the hem of her short white belted kimono, its back emblazoned with a vividly embroidered dragon. With one graceful twist she took a lotus position on Libby's carpet beside my cot.

"Yasmin, please turn the thing off." I pulled myself against the wall. She was a good-natured girl and did as I asked, without protest. Silence did not prevail. The hammering and the digging were in progress outside my square window. "What are they doing out there?" I groaned. She didn't understand my new objections. The cacophonous activities of the workmen were a disturbance she no longer noticed.

"You need your tea," she told me, and went to the door and called out loud and clear for Fatima; then back to the carpet in one delirious pirouette. "Today, after our midday rest, we will go to swim in the Caspian. Do you like to swim, Hope? I do not like to swim so much. The water frightens me, and the Caspian is very dangerous, though it deceives all with its calm. There will be people and fun at Nassrim's villa, and we will dine there tonight if you wish. My cousin Prince Bahram has appointed me your hostess, and it is my pleasant duty to make you happy while he is gone." She was glowing with pride.

"Did the prince already leave?" Had he looked in during the night and left me to my sweet dreams? A feeling of bereavement swept over me.

"He left so early he did not want to disturb you and asked me to extend his greetings. My cousin loves you very much, Hope. And so, too, does my uncle Karim." She twinkled at me. She rolled her golden eyes. "He is so crazy for women it is a little joke in our family. His wife was not so happy." Her eyes rolled again. "Always other women in other countries. My uncle Karim came to visit me in London where I was staying in my uncle Mehdi's English home, in Regent's Park. Do you like London, Hope? I do not like London too much—always so dark and rainy. And the men, they are not like my uncle Karim—so cold, so distant. I did not know ever what was inside their minds. The men of Ustan have one thing in their minds." She let out a rippling trill of a laugh.

She was courteous this morning to Fatima and jumped up to relieve her of a big round tray laden with two glasses and a bowl holding chunks of brown sugar, and another of honey, and flatbread and white cheese inside a white napkin, and a silver dish of walnuts and another of green herbs. Fatima ran out and came back with a samovar on another round tray.

"This is an Ustanian breakfast," Yasmin explained, holding the glass under the spigot of the bubbling samovar. "Do you want sugar or honey? The honey comes from mountains over to the east, where the emir has his summer palace. How lucky my cousin is to be invited so often. Our emir is very like my uncle Karim. How he loves the women." She babbled on, handing me the steaming glass of tea. "He has many foreign women. His wife, our empress, who knows Nassrim well, is not so happy with her life. There is rumor that the emir has taken another secret wife, very young and blond, and when he is in Switzerland, she is kept hidden in his private apartments. I do not think I will care, when I am old, if my husband takes a younger woman because he will be old, too, and I will have my sons to love"—her eyes twinkled—"and maybe the sons of other old ladies." Her laugh this time was almost raucous. She waited until I lit up before venturing to ask for a cigarette and almost consumed the luscious thing in one giant swallow of smoke.

"What are the workmen doing?" I persisted in my research during what could have been a blessed moment of silence.

She shrugged. "I do not really understand their work so well. My cousin Prince Bahram could better explain to you. He has told me, but it is so difficult for me. Under this old palace are many tunnels which our ancestors used to make the rooms up above more cool. It is these tunnels the workmen are repairing. My cousin Prince Bahram is a very wise, a very educated man—educated in your country, too, Hope—and it is his wish to make this palace as it was in our glorious past." She leaned close to me, her black hair moving like a satin drape around her face. "I am, of course, very proud of Ustan's glorious history—we were an old, a noble civilization—but to me, it is better and not without respect to the past to cool these rooms with the modern machines that make everything so nice and cold. What are they called, Hope?"

I told her. She rolled a piece of flatbread around a chunk of cheese, studded it with walnuts and the green grass from the silver plate, and all but fed it into my mouth. Not wanting to offend the child hostess, I took a small bite and found the concoction surprisingly delicious.

"How silly of me," she said, "to talk and talk like a chatterbox when there are so many things I want to know about your country. Tell me, Hope, is it true, there is a street called Madison Avenue, where shoes from France and Italy and now Brazil and Spain can be found? Oh"—she bit into a walnut half—"I want so much to go to New York. But as Nassrim has instructed me, I must be patient. At the end of the next month, only six weeks away, Nassrim will take me for my first visit to Paris. My uncle Mehdi did not permit me to travel out of London except to see the pretty country." She made a disgusted face.

From outside my window, over all the din, came the high-pitched cry I recognized as the call to prayer. By the time the last of the cries had faded away, the banging and the hammering had ceased. I could gladly have thrown myself on my face in a prostration of gratitude.

Yasmin revealed an irreligious temperament. "They are always praying," she said impatiently. "Pray, pray, pray—they do not give Allah a moment's peace." She laughed at her witticism. "Are you religious, Hope? I did not like the mullahs of my faith. They are all so dark and stern and hate everything that is pretty. My dead mother's father was a very famous mullah, higher than all the other mullahs, and he forced my mother to marry my father, who was the brother of Prince Bahram's mother's uncle. My father, who had been a general and a great warrior, died very young, of opium, I have heard, and my mother was returned with me to her father's house, which is in a dry place, in the middle of the desert." Yasmin shuddered. "I have no father to be returned to." She giggled some more and, noticing the silence, switched on her ghetto box and danced for joy. "You must excuse me now, Hope," she begged of me, which I found relatively easy to do. "I have my duties with Abbas." Her face went momentarily sullen. "I allowed you to sleep till quite late, and now it is time for his lunch. After we have rested, I will come and take you to Nassrim's." And she, and the music, and the hammering, and the digging were gone.

I drank my tea, prepared a couple more breakfast hors d'oeuvres, and inspected some of the gifts Yasmin had sneaked into the mirrored wardrobe and draped over the wall hooks during my recent bout with exhaustion. I bathed in the short curved tub and this time did not bother shampooing my hair with the aid of the hand-held shower.

There was another cry to prayer before she returned to my room, the silent radio gripped under her arm. She was wearing a species of caftan, more a smock, that reached mid-calf, and she brought a similar garment for me. She was quite astonished to discover there was no bathing suit included in my ravishing black trousseau. How could anyone come to the Caspian Sea so ill equipped? She found me a French maillot, which I chose over the teeny bikinis she preferred. She sat on my cot and watched as I nakedly wrestled with the flesh-colored elasticized knit, admiring my form and anticipating the enraptured disintegration of her beloved uncle Karim. She advised me to take along a deep purple straight-cut cotton gown, with tiny mirrors embroidered around the low slashed neckline, in case we remained all of the evening at Nassrim's.

And so, for the first time since I'd passed through the high front gate, I made my exit with Yasmin, accompanied by a carefully covered servant holding Abbas in her arms. The tall red-brick wall was no more than a few yards back from the shelf the palace was built on, separated by a deep ravine from another mountain on the other side. There were peasants seated on the ground, leaning against the wall, and Yasmin did not stop to speak to them.

"They are so foolish not to notice the prince's car is gone," she told me as we marched down the stone stairway. I saw, parked at the foot of the stairs, what I hadn't noticed the night I arrived, a yellow Land-Rover, facing away from the mountain. "This is the hour," she explained, "when Prince Bahram receives his villagers, who come to him with their problems."

"I see," I said as I climbed into the high leather seat beside her, the servant and Abbas on a pull-down seat in the rear.

"Prince Bahram is so good, so kind to his peasants," she commented, expertly operating the stick shift. "He has such patience with them. He says they are as dear to him as Abbas."

"Wonderful," I said, and hung on as Yasmin negotiated the Rover over a pitted roller coaster of a road. I didn't remember arriving on this many bumps and sharp curves, and I certainly hadn't been aware of the village on the right-hand side of the road we were now bouncing past. It was picturesque as only primitive can be, a series of squat, windowless, adobelike structures, all gathered around a hard-packed clearing, with lots of kids running around, and some children being carried by children not much larger. I saw women without veils there, and men seated in small circles, and chickens and dogs—it all looked very friendly. As we progressed, I noticed, in the evenly laid fields, women picking whatever they were picking and filling baskets hung on their stooped backs, their heads protected from the sun, though the worst of the sun's rays had burned during the siesta break.

We turned off that road to a much better one and went directly into and through a more sizable and commercial town that even had stores, and a mosque with a beautiful deep blue dome, and an open market; and at the edge of the town, just off the road, smiling women were chatting in a big sewing circle, except they were weaving a rug mounted on a big square frame.

The final turn was at the high, closed gates of Nassrim's villa. We waited there till servants pushed open the metal portals, with the screams and cries the slightest activity excited in them. Yasmin parked under a shading tree behind the villa. We walked 'round to the front, and we were at the Caspian Sea. There wasn't a ripple on the surface of the water; it stretched out, a dark blue-black green, into a flat and endless horizon.

Nassrim's villa was nothing to write home about. It took up a lot of space, but it was very plain, one story high and all white, its only remarkable feature a semicircular terrace that extended onto a strip of flat, hard-packed beach between it and the quiet water.

I could see right off how fond Nassrim was of her ward as she hugged her and greeted her with a few French-style cheek kisses. Nassrim was a stately, erect, full-figured woman, very simple in her attire. She was wearing, to be perfectly frank, an awful print housedress, and her hair was wrapped in a bandanna, as if she were one of the servants. On her feet were laced oxfords, and she even had on orangy-colored cotton stockings. The dowager-type woman had to be fifteen or twenty years older than the prince, and she'd been seated at a small table under an overhanging ledge that held a rolled-up awning, sorting through a pile of grass similar to the herbs served with my breakfast. Who should be beside her but Uncle Karim, who I had assumed was safely in the shadow of the emir's brilliant light. Effusive doesn't begin to describe how much happier he was to find himself in my shadow. He spoke to Nassrim in French, a language in which I was sufficiently conversant to follow the praises being sung on my behalf. Nassrim was cordial and polite, and though she looked directly at me, I had the strange sensation that the space I occupied was empty as far as she was concerned.

Two young men came charging from the beach onto the terrace, waved at us, picked up a wooden oar, and ran right back into the water to rescue a capsized Sunfish.

There were small, brightly striped square tents set up on the dark sand, and it was into one of these that Yasmin and I crawled to protect our complexions from the dire effects of the enemy sun. She had much more skin to protect than I, hardly an inch of her covered by the string bikini under her modest smock. What she desired, as we reclined, side by side, on rush mats, a flap of the tent tied back to let in the sea breezes, was for me to narrate the story of my life. That I lived alone was so staggering, so unimaginable a punishment to her that she stopped plucking the stray hairs she was idly tweezing from her smooth legs, to beg me to accompany her to Paris, dependent, of course, on Nassrim's consent. She had never spent a single solitary day out of the company of one of her relatives. She urged me to find a husband to replace the one I was so unwilling to discuss. She was sure he must have made me suffer terribly, as her own mother had suffered, as, to be more current, the American wife of the prince had suffered.

Yasmin had met Joanne on a few occasions, unfortunately before the broadening experience of London, and had been too young to form an opinion. Prince Bahram would not speak on the matter except—and I should forgive her for what she was about to say—to tell her that American women, even one as good and correct, as worthy of respect as his absent wife, were so lacking in traditional wisdom, so confused in their ignorance they had all lost the gift of peace and harmony, and out of their pain came discord and disorder. Yasmin pondered over the prince's statement. The prince was a sophisticated and traveled man, and she but a silly girl, going for the very first time to Paris, but when he spoke of peace and harmony, it was like listening to the words written in a holy book. She did not understand them. She did understand how a man and wife should be and how each had certain rights and domain under the rule of the emir. Was that what the prince meant by peace and harmony? Did American women have no rights? Was that why I had suffered the cruel excesses of my husband?

I said I was eager to test my new bathing suit in the Caspian. Yasmin came to the water's edge and went no farther. She issued a barrage of warnings about the treacherous unseen currents. She told me how many countless swimmers had drowned, two she had known personally. She felt that as a foreigner I must be told that there were creatures hidden in the depths that could burn and sting and even kill. She mentioned the harmful effects of the salt on the hair, as well as the lethal effects of swallowing it, and watched with horror as I made the suicidal plunge.

The Caspian was a tepid, shallow lake, and I had to swim out pretty far to reach a depth where I couldn't touch the bottom. I floated there, looking up at the thickly overgrown mountains, and nearer to me, on the road just above Nassrim's villa, I caught glimpses of black-veiled figures, peering down as they skittered by, like shades out of the dead past.

In Nassrim's villa I made a delightful discovery. There was electricity to burn, so to speak, and after my heroic dip, I was able to take a luxurious shower and shampoo and blow-dry my hair with a dryer Nassrim sent a servant to find.

The dinner, eaten at regulation-height tables set up on the terrace, was a jolly affair. Besides Nassrim and her husband—a man smaller than she, by profession an ambassador—and the two young beach bums, who, as it developed, were Nassrim's sons home on vacation from their French colleges, and Karim, of course, and Yasmin, and even Abbas, in his place, there were at least fifteen other dinner guests, many staying at Nassrim's villa and some wandering over from their own nearby villas. Karim couldn't have been more helpful, not unless he chewed my food and transferred it directly into my mouth. It developed he was as addicted to the habit of promenade after dinner as after the midday meal.

"Come with me for a refreshing stroll along the water, Hope," he suggested while pulling back my chair. Nassrim called out something to him in the language that had prevailed all through the tumultuous meal, and he waved aside whatever it was she had said. "You were so charming tonight, so patient at the table conversation that must have been so tedious for you, Hope." He reached into the breast pocket of his blazer to pull out a cigarette case. The sky was absolutely riddled with stars, and the air that touched my skin felt like suede.

"It wasn't tedious," I said, accepting one of his offered cigarettes. He stopped as he clicked a gold lighter and held the flame out for me and then himself.

"It was," he corrected me. "If I translated for you, you would know precisely how tedious. It's all gossip and an attempt to interpret the every action and word of the emir. Over there"—he pointed out a white house with lights within a patch of trees—"is the house that was once mine and is now my son's. Did you like my son, Hope?"

"Of course," I said.

"He is a very good man. They are all worried now, all of my family, about your good friend Prince Bahram."

"Really?" I said, and he had my attention.

"We know why the emir has sent for him. Our ruler is determined to build a hotel along this coast; he envisions the Caspian as a thriving resort, our very own Côte d'Azur." Karim chuckled. "You must promise me you will visit my modest shack in Antibes."

I promised. "And does the emir want Prince Bahram to build the hotel?"

"In a sense, he does," Karim said, after a bit of reflection. "You see, all of this coast is the property of my nephew, and by our new constitution, the emir may not build without a landowner's agreement. This my nephew has been foolishly reluctant to grant. We are worried—at least his sister is extremely worried—that he will persist in this futile resistance. He must agree," Karim said with an annoyed shrug.

"Why," I said, "if it's his land?"

Karim shook his gray head. "It is an interesting aspect of the Ustanian people's character to be ruled by absolute monarchs, and this one, with all his decrees and infatuation with modernization, may be the most absolute monarch of them all, the one who will tear this all down. I can quite appreciate my nephew's feelings. He is one of the few aristocrats who chose to live on their lands, and naturally he wants no intervention. His sister is afraid that her brother, virtually raised abroad, is as ignorant of our realities as any other foreign arrival." Karim adjusted the flapping skirts of my robe and rotated his thumb on the elbow it held.

"What could the emir do to Babi?"

"Babi? You mean the prince? I would not worry my head over this issue that should be of no concern to you. You are not here to share our worries but to share our festivities."

"But I do care. What could he do?"

"How fortunate my nephew is to have in you so dedicated a friend. Do you have anyone in New York, Hope, who is of special importance to you, someone who perhaps deserves your concern?"

"No," I said, "no one." And I almost blurted out the rest.

"A beautiful woman like you? It does not seem possible." He flirted. We locked eyes. "American men must be blind. Or is there no American man worthy of you? It is not so easy to find a real man anywhere, but in America it is probably the most difficult—perpetual children. A woman has no sense of what it could mean to be properly cared for, entirely safe, fully protected." His tribesman eyes gleamed at me. "How women flower when they are so treated! What anger and confusion fall away. I have seen it with my own French friend Nicole, whom I believe I mentioned in the garden." He was leading me back toward the gaily lit terrace. Rock music drifted our way.

I nodded.

"She became a flower for me." His hand swept my back. "But a flower has its moment of perfect bloom, and then it is gone. In you, Hope, I see a woman a bit mature but nevertheless at the height of her bloom."

He led me back onto the terrace. Yasmin was waiting, and Abbas was asleep in his nursemaid's arms. We got back into the yellow Land-Rover and did the uphill ride. There was no glowing watchman's fire on the crow's nest that night. Was it possible the palace was guarded only when the prince was there?

That first day set the pattern of the weeks that followed. Yasmin would enter my room and sit with me, expressing her ideas while smoking her head off. With the prince's return a day later, there was, of course, the hearty lunch in his court-yard, promptly followed by the obligatory siesta, with servants dropping on the spot, falling under trees, lying across door-ways, stretched out in cool corridors, as if the entire palace had been felled by an enchantment. Yasmin would fetch me for the hurtle over to Nassrim's, where we might, or might not, have dinner. The prince avoided the family get-togethers. He pre-ferred the solitary splendor of his summit. On occasion we might dine at Prince Bahram's palace, and there could be guests present, and those evenings would end with the en-trancing recitation by a hired reader, reading in a steady chant the prince's favorite poets, an entertainment that never failed to send his noisy family into a silent thrall.

I was content just to be there, secure in the knowledge that my presence was the prince's consolation. I discovered my role the day the prince returned from the thieving emir and opened his heart to me.

Of course, I was thrilled to see him when he returned from his perilous mission, and at lunch I asked him how things had gone with the emir. Babi was gloomy. "You would not under-stand, Hope," he told me.

"I would, Babi, I just know I would. When haven't I under-stood you?"

He sighed. "I do not know, Hope, if there is a greater pain than being subject to the control of a willful and limited man."

I gave him my tiniest smile.

"I, of all people, who lived most of my life in the West, am being accused of backwardness, as if I do not see clearly how these pockets of progress will tear my country apart. What are they doing but stirring up false appetites?"

"Who?" I said, striving to keep up with him. "Who's doing the stirring?"

"Let's talk later, Hope," the prince said, his suffering written all over his face. "We haven't really had time for a talk. Would you mind, this afternoon, waiting till I am finished with my duties—you understand, I was not available to my villagers yesterday. But as soon as I am finished, I'll come for you."

"Babi, take as much time as you need. When have I ever not been there for you when you asked me to wait?" And Yasmin and Abbas left for Nassrim's without me.

What long hours princes put in! I waited in my chamber, dressed in the white silk caftan that had been Yasmin's personal gift. I waited till there were no more workmen sounds and the light coming in through my grated window was darker than even the darkness in the room. A servant finally came for me and took me to the prince, who was impatiently pacing at the arcade of branches leading to the garden I had visited on my first day.

Side by side, in our white robes, Babi and I walked into the garden. He held a thick staff in his hands and wore thick-soled sandals and really looked like a young Moses. I couldn't repress an internal chortle at imagining what a sensational hit we'd make on St. Mark's Place. He'd have to fight the cultists off with his stick.

To my surprise, Babi did not take me to the double swing but pressed on through the garden past a wall of high poplars, and continued walking, till I realized we were on the meandering path to the structure up above, the deck sailing out of the mountain. The climb got steeper, and the stones got harder, and before long I was catching my breath in sobbing gasps. Babi, in the lead, was a mountain goat, a mountain sprite, jumping to the next level and looking back at me. He held out his staff and pulled me abreast of him at the bottom of the wooden structure. There was a ladder slanting up from the ground to the deck.

"Those pernicious cigarettes, Hope." He wagged a teasing finger at me.

My legs were trembling. I decided to preserve whatever breath was left in me for the climb up the ladder. I stepped out on the wooden deck and saw it wasn't the spare space I had pictured. There was a rug on the wood floor and a railing around the deck, with backrests and cushions. A charcoal brazier was there, and it, at least, answered to my expectations. And there was a lot of other paraphernalia, trays, and a bubbling samovar, previously delivered by a thoughtful sprite. Babi took hold of a thick cord hanging off the mountain and rolled the lowered awning up, as if he were removing the roof from the earth to expose the entire sky. It was a spectacular panorama.

"Babi!" I exclaimed. "Babi! How incredible!" It was like standing on the edge of the infinite. A mighty wave of vertigo forced me to my knees.

"It's wonderful here, isn't it?" The prince was justifiably proud of the surprise he'd sprung on me.

"I don't know if I could be up here alone," I said in all honesty. I cautiously peeked down through the railings, and there was the palace, all laid out, small as a doll's palace. I could see where the workers had gouged out the earth, and the ribbon of a garden that had seemed so grand.

"It is the only place where I am able to be alone, the only place I can be unobserved, be with myself." He lowered himself to a rug beside me, supporting himself against a cushion.

I looked up at the sky. It wasn't dark. It was streaked a million colors you never see unless you get that close. I saw stars come out that were not yet visible below.

"There were porches like this all over Ustan in the Middle

Ages," Babi said, "but the peasants tore them down for the use of the wood. This one was left mostly intact, though it required a lot of work to secure it to the mountain."

"I bet it did," I said.

He laughed his deep, throaty laugh. "Little did you know," he said, "what you were getting into when you picked up a shy, cringing student. Wasn't I a jerk?"

"You were okay, Babi. Kindly do not cast aspersions on my impeccable perception. I took one look at you, and I thought: That guy is a prince."

"Well," he said fondly, "then you saw something I hadn't seen yet. But now, Hope, it is true. I am a prince, and what a strange thing it is to be. If not for you, I wonder if I'd have escaped for those few years from this thing I was going to be."

"There's something I always wanted to tell you, Babi, and this would be as good a moment as any. If not me, there would have been someone else. You were a pretty hot number."

He laughed some more. He was busying himself removing a flat metal box stored between two piled-up cushions. He opened the box and set it next to his thigh. Inside were tongs and long needles and a tightly screwed jar that contained an aluminum-wrapped cigar-shaped object.

"I like to smoke a few pipes of opium up here." He explained his actions. "Will you smoke with me, Hope? It is not necessary if you'd rather not."

I felt a rush of fear. Really, I was quite high enough up there. If I got any higher, would my darling remember to get me down? There were a few unimportant but curiously persistent remembrances of a few occasions when he'd neglected to do so.

He let me decide for myself while he lit the prepared charcoal brazier. A blue flame shot straight up into the sky, and after that the sky was completely dark.

Babi slipped the bowl and stem of a pipe out of their flannel pouches and reassembled the parts. Then he took a sharp instrument and shaved off raisin-sized pellets of opium from the gummy brown stick he had removed from its wrapping. He smoked the first pipeful, catching a glowing coal in long tongs and melting the opium into the pinhole on the bowl of the pipe; and the sounds of his sucking in the smoke were the only sounds in the universe. He fixed himself another pipe and leaned against the backrest to smoke it.

He fixed another pipe, and I said, "Babi, I'd really like to try one."

I held the stem to my lips while Babi carefully placed one of the pellets on the bowl, and it was interesting to watch it boil and sizzle and flow like lava into the pinhole and end up as a stream of sweet smoke ballooning inside my lungs. I smoked another pipe, and another. I lay back on a cushion and held up the sky with the tip of my nose.

"Are you all right?" he asked me. His voice was drowsy, languid. God, did it stir up memories.

"I'm fine." My voice was fuzzy.

"I never could bring Joanne up here," he said with a really wistful sigh. "I've been thinking and thinking about her, and thinking of the ways I failed her. Poor girl. I'm afraid she was never intended to have such a difficult life."

"Difficult?" I listened to my word float off into the firmament.

"Terribly difficult. She's suffered, Hope. And it is my pain that there is nothing I could or can do to relieve or change it. This is where her path took her. Fate is not always fair."

"Babi . . ." I began to berate him, but it was so hard not to just lie there and listen, even if he was foolishly beating on himself.

"How could she not suffer? An American girl in love with a couple of half-baked ideas, a girl with almost no inner resources, comes to a place like this to live with a man like me.

My wife is a megaphone, shouting back at the world whatever she hears it shout at her. And she comes to this silence where nothing she has to say is of the slightest importance. None of us is important, but at least most of us fill the roles we must fill. Joanne, however, was not suited to fill hers."

It wasn't necessary to talk. It never is when you finally hear someone speaking your mind.

"Her role here is intimately connected to who I am. That is how she is seen. That is who she is. Her role, in a sense, Hope, is to make the sacrifices to me that I am obliged to make to my people. Can you understand that?"

"A sacrifice, Babi, is only as good as the sacrificer." Some drugs are amazing. They just hold up flash cards of wisdom inside your closed lids.

"Joanne is a very good woman, Hope. I admire and respect her basic goodness. I admire and respect the suffering she has borne for five whole years. If only she would learn something from it and not continue to divide what is right from what is wrong, judging, evaluating what she cannot comprehend. If only her suffering could make her surrender this shallow view, it would be such an awakening for her."

"Ahh," I said.

"I've learned so much, Hope, from returning to my home, to my people. I see the suffering my peasants endure. They go without so much you can't imagine. Hundreds and hundreds of our villages have no doctor, no teacher, no electricity." He gurgled a laugh inside his throat. "And they are so beautiful in their suffering. The dignity, the certainty you see in their eyes. I love how bravely they embrace their pain."

"How nice for them," I said.

"And that, my dear, is the end of the lesson of what it means to be a prince."

"What? What?" Were we leaving?

He was fixing himself another pipe. My heart settled down.

"I am not a personal man any more. These peasants who suffer need someone to be their witness, to observe their pain, to reassure them and be there for them as a parent, as a father must be."

"And who is there for you, Babi? Who is your witness? Who is there to care about your pain?" I absolutely could not discern if I had said those words aloud or only inside my head.

"Do you want another pipe, Hope? One for the road?"

"But it's so beautiful here. Why are we leaving?"

"It's late," he told me. "You must get the rest you came here to get."

"Not yet, Babi. Please. Lie down next to me." To my ever-lasting happiness the prince complied. He settled back on his pillow, and I lay spread-eagled under the low sky. "Remember when you used to tell me that you were the sky and I was the earth?"

"No, Hope, dearest." His mouth was brushing my ear. "You always rearrange everything. I told you I was the *sun* and you were the earth. It is a famous image from one of our classical poets." He stroked my cheek and scratched my scalp. "You're still so great-looking," he continued in his sultry voice. "Do you have a secret formula, Hope?"

"Suppose I do."

He laughed.

"Babi," I softly said, "isn't it lonely for you up here? From my window it looks so lonely."

"Yes, it's lonely. I'm accustomed to loneliness. It was that you spared me for a brief moment in New York, the loneliness that was waiting here for me."

"I'm lonely, too," I quickly confessed. "I can't tell you *how* lonely. Babi, why did we separate? Why did we part after the miracle of coming together from opposite sides of the world?"

"Hope, dear, we never parted. This is our proof. That you are here still sharing my heart and my home."

"Of course." His face was over mine, blocking out the sky. He was the sky. The classical poet was wrong.

He reached down for me. "Come on, Hope, you're zonked." His white teeth glinted in the darkness. I locked my fingers behind his neck, and we may have pulled in opposite directions. His soft beard brushed my cheek, and his lips, full of the sweet scent of opium, grazed mine. I drew in a long, sweet draft of his breath and floated to the calm center of the storm.

"Don't bliss out." The prince was shaking me as if to keep me awake. "Let me take you down now, Hope." I offered him no resistance. He held me close to him till we reached the courtyard of the women's quarters.

In the nights becoming unhurried weeks that followed, I'd sit on my cot, sipping at the Rémy Martin, keeping vigil with him over the charcoal fire with such an intensity my darling Babi had to feel once again that he wasn't alone.

12

The prince, Karim informed me during one of our by now customary constitutionals along the sea, had until the end of August to volunteer the desired strip of beachfront to the Exalted and Merciful and Progressive Emir. It was a sign of the marvelous advancement of the monarchy that Babi had withheld his definite consent and still enjoyed the mobility of all his limbs. I shuddered for my darling as I had shuddered in the past when he threw himself bodily against the forces of capitalist militarism—brave, reckless pawn of integrity that he was.

My ardent and elderly admirer filled me in on the prince's economic situation. He had more land than anyone else in his family since many of them had foolishly sold theirs at irresistible profits and some had lost valuable real estate as the result of the emir's beneficent land reform acts. Babi's obstinacy had his relatives in a stew. I sometimes wondered if it was that multitudinous pack he was defying and not just the greedy emir. Babi certainly frowned on the family's crude adoption of Western ways as evidenced at Nassrim's villa.

The prince's family flocked in droves to the Caspian, and more precisely, to Nassrim's, for their traditional summer summit, and though a sprinkling of the elders retained a fierce and foreign tribesman demeanor, on the whole they were the well-dressed, well-fed VIP international set dedicated to elevating play to new heights. I could see them through the prince's clear vision, and what I saw did not impress me. Nassrim's sons were gripped by one subject: the necessity of laying a tennis court on their mother's property. When they weren't playing with their boats, they played with their Frisbees, they played with their hi-fi equipment, they played with each other, dancing up a storm on the back patio. And the women combed the remote mountain villages, snatching up rugs and handwoven cloths and prized antiquities as if the whole country were their kleptomaniac paradise. What a contrast between the prince's serene palace and the pirates at the villa below. Nassrim, like her princely brother, had no taste for acquiring things, though she certainly was not going to deprive her beloved sons. However, she did have one small personal extravagance—horses. She and the Queen of England were in compulsive correspondence on the subject of foaling. Babi was never critical of his elder sister, who was a good twenty years his senior and a species of surrogate mother. There was a middle sister mysteriously hospitalized in Switzerland, and the wide age differences were attributable to previous exiles, separations, assassinations, and banishments. The prince had hardly known his parents, world wanderers buried now in distant climes.

"Babi," I spoke into his deepening silence one afternoon at lunch, "I agree with you that the emir has one colossal nerve helping himself to your land, but you have so much of it. Is that one little piece you can't even see from here worth all your worry and anxiety?"

He lifted a sorrowful countenance. "I appreciate your concern for me, Hope, but it is not for myself that I resist the emir. How can I permit a vulgar hotel to be stuck right in the middle of my peasants' hardships? It's an insult, a provocation to them. The summer months, with the invasion of surfers and boaters and swimmers, is difficult enough; now, must there be a hotel that could make the invasion a year-round catastrophe?"

The prince was counting the days when his revered family would pack it in and move the Caspian caravan on. He waited for the time when only he would remain on his lofty pinnacle, and I waited for and with him. The weather itself, so unfailingly bright for the first few weeks, began to reflect the prince's solemn mood. The skies got overcast. The palace darkened. And Yasmin's vibrancy dampened. She got petulant and pouty, and one of my services to the prince, one of my private ways of preserving his oasis of peace, was to cheer up the frivolous girl. I'd listen for endless hours to her ever-approaching sacking of the city of Paris. She was counting days, too, marking them off on a big wall calendar pinned above her cot. As breathlessly as she anticipated her departure, I anticipated for and with her. Her conversations on the subject of shoes and dresses wore me down, and more and more I retreated to my chamber to commune with my bountiful inner resources. Deep as I dug into those fabulous resources, they would not yield a letter to Marshall Springer. I'd been toiling at one since the day I'd arrived at the palace or, at most, by the following week. Maybe that final airport shot of Marshall's sourpuss was intervening because I never could get further than half a page. I tried in one to be funny about the scene at the Inter-Continental, and it came out sounding as amusing as a night on death row. Another pen-pal effort of mine on the subject of Yasmin's arsenal had all the humor of a letter dictated by Karl Marx. It was weird to end up incapable of even sending a simple hello to my mentor.

Abbas haunted my room. His greatest pleasure, like his father's before him, was to cuddle up to me in bed and lie there in enraptured silence as I read from the books Joanne was sending to her son. Joanne. As the weeks went by I forgot she'd ever existed. Only these big, brightly illustrated tracts on girl engineers and boys raising babies produced fleeting images of the unsuitable princess.

Yasmin came less often to wile away the mornings since exhausting our cigarette stock. But I kept my nightly vigil, and these were the hours of my deepest restoration, so it was jarring, to say the least, to have Yasmin come bounding into my room, yelling over the deafening volume at which she played her favorite Sex Pistols cassette.

"Hope, the most wonderful news! Prince Bahram has consented to drive us to the bazaar at Baijan, which is the largest bazaar of all these tedious little mountain villages."

"Really?" I lifted myself up on my elbow.

"Oh, Hope, what is the matter with you? You have become so lazy. Always I find you in this bed alone or reading to that naughty boy Abbas."

I looked up and out of the window. It was grayer than the recent succession of grays. "Why do you want to go to a bazaar?" I foolishly asked.

She became positively adamant. "I must buy presents to take with me at the end of this week, to Paris. I must bring gifts for my aunts and uncles and cousins who have been so generous to me and brought so many pretty things to the Caspian."

My head fell back on the pillow. Three more days of her. Would I make it?

"And Prince Bahram," she happily rattled on, "wishes to visit the mosque at Baijan, which is of the greatest antiquity and holiness, Hope; really, you must see some of the wonders of my country. It is not good of my dear cousin Prince Bahram to neglect his duties as a host. There is much he could take you to see that would be of great interest to you. We are leaving soon." She danced to the frantic music. "We will have lunch in a caravansary—very famous, very beautiful—in the town of Baijan. Hurry, Hope. Hurry, please. Prince Bahram is waiting."

But he wasn't waiting. He had actually appeared at my door.

"Perhaps Hope would rather stay here by herself, Yasmin."

"But why would she stay here all alone?" Yasmin whirled around at him. She had on a long, sheer skirt and a long-sleeved tunic top, obligatory covering if she wished to enter the mosque. "You are not correct to your guest." Yasmin let fly at her cousin. "It cannot be entertaining for a woman so intelligent as Hope to have always only a silly girl such as me to talk to. And now that she may have a day to buy pretty gifts, you tell her to stay alone?" The girl was outraged.

"Not everyone, Yasmin, is as eager to accumulate these roomfuls of wasteful things that are so necessary to your happiness."

They were addressing each other in English, for my benefit, of course. It sounded strange, as if they were speaking a private language way over my head.

"But I must have my things!" the girl violently expostulated.

Babi showed me a harried visage. This scene was all he needed, with the emir breathing down his neck. I tried to decode the message in his soft and beautiful eyes.

"Actually, Yasmin, I think I would prefer to stay here."

I'd read him right. His features imperceptibly lightened. He needed the reassurance that there was someone in his corner, someone who shared his view of life.

For the very first time in the weeks and weeks we'd spent together, both of us pulling the Paris departure closer and closer, as if we were transporting a barge, Yasmin directed anger at me.

"I thought you would be interested to see more of my country, Hope. I am sorry if I have disturbed your rest." And so saying, she briskly left the room.

"Forgive her." Babi quickly bent over me. "She's a child. She doesn't understand that these trivial events important to her do not hold the same charm for us." *Us!*

"It's not necessary for you to apologize for Yasmin, Babi. I like her, a lot." I touched his hand.

"I've been meaning to thank you, Hope, for being so kind to her. And so patient and comforting to Abbas." His face tightened and then just as quickly relaxed. "This might be the opportunity I've been waiting for to thank you. Is there anything you want, anything special I could bring you?"

"How about a perfect rose?" I suggested, and we both cracked up. I could always make *us* laugh.

I must have dipped into those inner resources of mine because the next thing I knew I was all but levitated off the bed by a palace-shaking clap of thunder. What a rain fell on the Elburz Mountains that day! It was torrential, waves and gusts of it. The sky was a churning ocean. Bolts of lightning lit up my room as though the generator of generators were operating. The rain fell all day and continued throughout the night. I thought the mountain would turn to mud and the palace would slide down into the primordial sludge below. At one point Fatima, shawl over her head, came in, carrying a covered tray, and set it beside my bed. It felt so good to be safe inside with all that havoc out there. And I wasn't waiting for anything. Everything was right there, everything I needed, even though there was no phone and no TV and no electricity and no cigarettes and not even any Rémy Martin. There was just me, listening to the lullaby of the rain, gliding through the dark, safe channel and sliding smoothly out into the light. But this was daylight, not the white blaze of the lightning.

Yasmin flung open my door. "Hope, I was so worried you had drowned here. Was it not a magnificent rain? Does it rain in such a way in America? Bahram and I could not do the return drive. It was so much fun to be in a big town such as Baijan. There they even have a restaurant. Come, come"—she was tugging at me, radiant with happiness—"you must come to see the fantastic gifts I have found in the bazaar."

I let her drag me out into the courtyard. The emptied sky was drained of all color, and the washed trees and bushes and grass were an iridescent, a phosphorescent green. The birds in the courtyard were clamoring about their survival. The door to Yasmin's sanctum was wide open, and men were staggering under sacks supported on their stooped backs, delivering Yasmin's purchases.

The prince appeared at the archway into the women's quarters. "Are you all right, Hope? Did you enjoy the rain? Wasn't it magnificent?" He was in an extraordinarily cheerful mood. It had been good for him to get away from the palace and his workers and his peasants and his family and his emir and, best of all, to find me there waiting for him. "Look at what that crazy girl has bought!" he affectionately urged me. "There's not a bead left in the Baijan bazaar." He shook his head in disbelief as another stooped man under another groaning sack staggered down the open passageway. "I will see you at lunch." Was he planning to give me the perfect rose then?

Yasmin was exultant in showing her purchases, which included, believe it not, a carton of Winstons cunningly concealed from the prince. She told me just how she'd managed her defiance, gleaming with pleasure, and it was a secret bond between us at lunch, where her exultation dimmed not an iota.

The palace got lively with the preparations for Yasmin's ecstatic exit. She packed up her belongings twenty-four hours a day, back and forth from the palace to Nassrim's. She must have made a hundred trips in the yellow Land-Rover. It was a phenomenal performance, second only to the cleansing storm. The countdown was picking up momentum—in five days, in four days, in three, tomorrow!

"Tomorrow, Hope! Tomorrow I will leave for Paris, but tonight you must be the most beautiful ever for the fete Nassrim makes in my honor."

It was comical to witness the importance she invested in her siege of Paris. She ran into my room uncountable times on the fete day to give me gifts, and more gifts, and a special, special gift. It couldn't be that big a fete, as the large clan had been thinning out steadily for the past week or two. The overcast weather had really got them moving back to their hotel suites in London and chalets in Switzerland and châteaus in France. My prince had to conceal the joy he felt in their departure, as one by one they'd mounted the stone steps to bid him adieu.

"What shall you wear tonight?" Yasmin asked me. She was at the foot of my bed, on Libby's rug, painting her toenails. She'd already finished painting mine. She'd also demanded an evening of electricity, and for the first time since my arrival I sat in a really lit room of the palace. Funny how I hadn't recognized the enameled wall sconces as electric lights.

"Yasmin, I don't know. You've given me so many gowns. Maybe I'll wear two of them." I jested with her. But she was talking serious business and frowned at my levity.

"But, Hope, it is as a compliment to me that you will be your most beautiful tonight. My dear friend, who has been so kind to me and so patient, and who I will always think of with the greatest respect and love—I could not have endured this gloomy old palace without you, Hope. I want my last picture of you, the one I will remember, to be a beautiful, a happy, fantastic Hope."

It was not to be believed!

Yasmin shampooed and hennaed my hair, and we plugged in my blow dryer, and she fussed over me and tweezed some unacceptable hairs from under my eyebrows. I began to feel more and more like one of those women you see being ritually prepared for a major ceremony. She selected the dress for me, of course.

"Givenchy," she said in a hushed whisper. "There is no one as good as Givenchy for the plain-cut evening gown." And with these assurances I accepted a pale gray, silvery, satin evening gown, cut close to the body, the shoulders and back and chest left bare, and a satin cape to cover the whole scandalous affair.

"And these, Hope." Yasmin held out a pair of silver sandals. She was actually giving me a pair of shoes. Shoes! I was so touched at the monumental sacrifice tears actually sprang to my eyes.

"You are too much, Yasmin," I said, and I hugged her hard because she had made my being in the palace easier for me. She had helped me to wait for the prince.

The sky was magnificent as the three of us—Babi at the wheel, Yasmin our irrepressible chaperone in the middle, and me at the window—drove to Nassrim's. The prince was very elegant tonight, in black trousers and a white jacket and a white shirt and a medallion instead of a tie. He wore on his feet velvet slippers, their tongues embossed with the gold heads of lions. Yasmin, to complete the rather sensational picture, was in a confection—peach chiffon ruffles, layers of them, from halfway up her breasts down to her ankles. She was also mortifying her flesh in stiletto-heeled black pumps that were out of this world.

Nassrim's villa was especially decorative that night, as a matter of fact. There were little lights strung in the flowering bushes and more little lights outlining the terrace, and the terrace was set with round tables and white chairs, and servants were carrying trays to a considerable crowd. Where had they all come from? One I instantly recognized came at me with the single thrust of a shark.

"Hope, you are so extraordinary this evening that I am ill at the very idea of leaving tomorrow and finding myself deprived of your beautiful face and your most enchanting company."

The prince gave me an approving look.

"May I fix you some caviar?" Karim implored, and took me to a table far from the prince. Yasmin was mingling, surrounded by her own admirers, mostly relatives who petted and doted on her.

I sat at the small table with Karim and realized I was hearing the efforts of a live musician, an old man in a black rumpled suit, sitting cross-legged on a carpet at the corner of the terrace, a stringed instrument across his lap. With small, rapidly moving mallets he was creating a high, whining, eerie, piercing sound.

Karim escorted me to the dinner being served in the rear patio. Buffet tables circled the patio, and shish kebab pits were burning at the side, and there were tables lit by small floating alcohol fires. Karim beside me moaned all through the dinner. "Tomorrow my life will be empty. Why do you stay on the Caspian? It will be too cold, too damp for you, Hope."

And the prince and Yasmin across the table, Babi indulgently observing his uncle, and Nassrim and the ambassador and their two *sportif* sons, and no one stopped talking or celebrating for one single moment. I watched Babi fold. I knew he was not long for this party.

Karim would have his last evening constitutional. He asked the prince if he might steal me away, and my darling encouraged the larceny. Karim lit our cigarettes—we had quite a few intimate habits—and I walked toward the moon and watched its reflection on the surface of the perfectly silent

water. We were silent, too. We both were probably listening to
the strains of the lone musician, whose sounds penetrated even
to here. I slipped off my silver sandals, and Karim promptly re-
lieved me of the burden, dangling them from his buffed fingertips. My footsteps were as silent on the sand as the moon was
on the water.

"Ah, Hope," Karim's lamentation began, "you are cruel not
to accept my Riviera invitation." My greatest summer triumph
had been to keep his ardor tightly reined. "You see here"—he
stopped me—"this is where our emir intends to build his
hotel." I dutifully looked at the empty space.

"If the prince grants his consent," I said with some pride.

"Are you serious, Hope? I took you to be more perceptive.
Of course, my nephew has already given his consent. That was
in part what our family was celebrating."

I peered at him in the darkness.

"Next time you return to our glorious shores," he continued, "and I pray there will be a next time, you may find a hotel
standing here, or, as is much more likely, half a hotel. Monarchs start many more projects than they complete." He
laughed.

"Well, I'm glad your nephew made a sensible decision."

"He had no choice, Hope. He has an illusion of choice, sitting up there on his mountain peak, as if he and it were unas-
sailable. Unfortunately"—Karim got grave—"there are no safe
mountain peaks in my country." He sighed. "Forgive my self-
absorption, dear Hope, it is only that I never leave my beloved
country without the deep fear in my heart that I will never see
it again."

"But of course you will." I put my hand on his sleeve.

"I'm not so sure. This monarch is for some reason denying
the true nature of our people, and doing so with too much
haste. It is producing unrest or eccentrics, like my intelligent
nephew, who believe they can create an entire universe of their

own. Well, at least he will have less unhealthy isolation in his universe with Yasmin there at his side. I wonder. I have not been sure all summer that the match is right, but Nassrim is positive. She says Yasmin is only a girl and she will see that this exuberance of hers is exercised now, and with a few children to occupy her, she may make Prince Bahram a splendid wife."

"What?" I knew then the meaning of *petrified.* I was petrified, frozen to the spot.

"What is the matter, Hope? Why this look of consternation?"

"Yasmin his wife?" The words fragmented into gibberish.

"But surely, Hope, you have been told. How very strange for you not to be told. Did you not know this party was in celebration of Yasmin's betrothal to Prince Bahram?"

The feeling that seized me was not easy to bear. The sea was calm, the sky was calm, the sand was not moving, and I was standing in an earthquake. I turned away from Karim and began to run toward the terrace into the music.

"Hope, wait, why are you running? Slow down. . . ." His voice pursued me. It made me mad. It made me run faster. He grabbed me as I was swinging myself onto the terrace. "Where are you going in this agitated state, my dear?"

"I want to see Babi!"

"Babi? Ah, Prince Bahram. You are angry that he neglected to take you into his confidence? It was very rude of him. I shall certainly discuss it with him if you like."

"I want to see him," I repeated, and tried to wrest my arm free. But Karim held on tight.

"The prince is no longer in there. He left the party when we went off on our walk."

I ran to where cars were parked. I was ready to steal one. Karim stayed at my side. "What are you doing?" the poor man appealed to me.

"I want to go home. I want to see him," I said.

"Of course. Whatever you wish. I will take you home immediately." And he motioned at a shadow that turned out to be a
chauffeur, and we got into Karim's Mercedes that smelled like
a leather glove, and I never answered a single one of his questions, till he threw up his arms and crossed his well-tailored legs
and leaned back into the seat, his arms folded over his chest, fed
up with the irrational female.

I jumped out as the car stopped. Karim stayed with me. The
man was prepared to track me to my grave.

"Your shoes," he said desperately, holding them up.

"Stay here," I ordered, and I flew up the stone steps barefoot,
and pulled the bell, and brought out the servants. I ran
through the room that led to the patio that led to the gardens
that led to the flying deck. I saw the red glow of his charcoal
fire.

I held my skirts high and hardly felt the stones as I labored
up the mountain and hauled myself up the ladder and heaved
my body onto the deck like a spent swimmer.

"Babi!"

"Hope, oh, my God, how you frightened me!" The prince
had changed into his at-home white robe, and he was on his
feet, ready to fend off whatever demon the sea had thrown up.

"Are you marrying Yasmin?" I bellowed at him.

"Hope!" He was dancing around me. "What is this hysteria,
this scene, here of all places?"

"Answer my question!" I roared.

"Why is it asked in such fury, such anger? To marry or not
to marry is my decision to make."

"You are marrying that child. It's true." I staggered back.
Nothing separated me from the void.

"Yes, it's true. Hope, compose yourself. I must marry. I cannot be without a wife. In my position a wife is a necessity."

"I see," I sneered at him. "Another sacrifice wrung from you.
Another duty you are obliged to perform. How you suffer,
Babi."

He cringed from the demonic sight of me. I closed in on him. "This is how you love your children. You fuck them. This is how you love your peasants. You fuck them. This is how you loved me. You fucked me. Is there no limit to the love you suffer?"

"You're mad. What is this madness, this detestation? What would you have me do? I wrote to Joanne. She knows of Nassrim's arrangements."

"Joanne knows?" I put my head back and howled at the moon. "You lied to me," I howled.

He grabbed my shoulders. "Hope, please. Please, my dear friend." He was whimpering, already claiming my pain! "When did I lie to you? What lie did I tell to you?"

"You've always lied. Every word you ever spoke to me was a lie. He broke my heart," I declaimed to the high heavens. I spun around wild as a dervish, and the stars spun even faster. I made a lunge for the railing, and Babi grabbed me and held onto both my arms to steady me. "Don't help me," I growled into his pale face etched with my pain. I went limp against his chest and wept as I have never wept since growing up.

After my crying jag I was able to negotiate the ladder independently. I trudged down the slope. It was so quiet there were no sounds but the deep internal tolling of my own grief. Had I ever heard it before? I broke into a run and ran the rest of the way to topple on my cot. It was awhile before I raised my eyes to the specter I had sat watch over all summer long. The embers glowed, and the tiny coal held in the tongs blinked on and off, on and off. Signal from a phantom ship. My heart ached. Beloved ghost. Fresh tears flowed. I stayed at my post till the flashes blurred and were suddenly gone in the brightness of dawn.

It was broad daylight in the room and there were noises in the corridor. I hadn't slept, but I didn't feel tired. I felt calm. It's very calming not to have one single thought. The noises got closer, and my door opened.

"Hello, Hope," Joanne said. She was holding Abbas trapped in her arms, and he was wiggling to escape.

I gaped at her. She was sporting her green shirtwaist, and the waist was not where it was supposed to be.

"That's a very beautiful gown," she said, stone-faced. "Have you been to a party?"

I laughed out loud. "Where are you coming from, stranger?"

"Hetron."

"Hetron?"

"I arrived last evening. The flight was five hours late, and there was nothing to be had at the hotel."

"Tell me," I said as I sat down on the edge of the cot.

Abbas got free of his mother and streaked out of the room.

"He's angry at me," she said with a sorrowful smile.

"He'll be all right. How did you get here?"

"I called Bahram's uncle Darius. Have you met him?"

I said I had.

"He gave me the use of his chauffeur and car. We drove right through the night." She paused and looked at me and started to say something and didn't say it and sat down alongside me. "Do you think I'm foolish, Hope, weak to come back to him this way? It is his child. . . ."

"Joanne," I said, "has it ever occurred to you that we have one single topic of conversation?"

She sighed. "Have you been having a good time?" she asked.

"Let's say I've already had it," I answered.

Fatima came in with a tray of tea, and Joanne consoled the emotional servant in her own language. The woman dabbed her veil at the corners of her eyes. She deposited the tray on the rug and, bending over, took hold of Joanne's hand and kissed it.

"My, my," I said, "you're a popular favorite around here." I glanced up at the slope. There was no sign of life from the becalmed ship.

"Has he been up there all night?" Her lips became prim.

"Who?"

"I received Bahram's letter concerning Yasmin a bit late," she repeated with indignation. "What a wonderful mother that adolescent would make for Abbas." She gave me a sidelong glance. "Marshall told me you were here. He drove me to the airport."

"I bet he did." I started to laugh. "What does he have, the concession driving Babi's wives to Kennedy?"

"He gave me something for you," she said, and as she spoke, she uncoiled a thin chain from around her neck, and hanging from it was a round crystal watch. "I wore it over." She handed me the trinket. "Marshall said you'd know where it came from."

"I do," I gurgled. Old Leo. Marshall still pimping for good old Leo. I hung it around my neck. I checked the magnified face. It said ten o'clock. "Is it already ten o'clock?"

"That's the time in New York. I didn't want to fiddle with it." She was leaning back, her expression exhausted, drinking the glass of tea so thoughtfully supplied by Fatima.

"Evening or morning?"

"Evening," she answered.

Ten in the evening. It was still last night in New York. Imagine, Marshall and I could be strolling down to the World Trade Center to aid the digestion of one of his disgusting home-cooked meals.

"What's the date?"

"I'm not sure." She was getting cranky, from either jet lag or motherhood. "It's either August thirty-first or September first. Why didn't you tell me you were coming here, Hope?"

"I swear, Joanne, I didn't know. I didn't know what I was going to do, with you busy having Libby condemned for her building."

Joanne rubbed her knuckles. "I dropped the litigation. I

never even began it," she admitted with a shrug. "I spoke to Libby before I left New York."

"Did you? Did you both make up?"

"I suppose so. She's been on the Cape all summer. She told me she'd been trying to reach you, but you're never home," Joanne dryly added.

Fatima came into the room, and she and Joanne exchanged a few words.

"Excuse me." The princess went all Ustanian on me. "Fatima was telling me Darius's chauffeur is ready to return to Hetron."

My pulses began to throb. "Tell him to wait, Joanne. Go tell him right now. I'm going back to Hetron with him."

"What? I just arrived. You can't leave like this. What would Bahram think?"

"Joanne, give me a break. I can't spend my whole life solving your marital problems. Don't tell me to stay, ask me to leave."

"This is crazy," she protested, but did as she was told.

I knew exactly what I had to do. I pulled the suitcase out from where it had been stashed during this marvelous holiday. I opened it and dumped all of the contents on the cot.

Joanne came back. "The chauffeur is waiting," she said, which has to be the greatest line an American woman can have addressed to her. My heart was pumping double time. I looked up at the suspended vessel. Signs of life. The lowering of the awning.

I knelt in my silver finery and asked Joanne please to get off the rug so I could fold it and get it into the valise. It was a perfect fit. So that's what the monster suitcase was designed for!

"Hope, please, don't be in such a hurry. There are much more beautiful rugs for you to take back with you."

"This one is beautiful enough for me."

I pulled off my silver sheath and was about to throw it on the black heap when I figured: Well, you never know when a well-cut Givenchy silver rag could come in handy. I poured it on top of the rug and closed the contraption. I passed on Yasmin's wondrous gifts. I pulled the navy blue linen marvel over my head and stepped into my sling-back sandals. The shoulder-strap bag was on the hook it was always on. I checked my passport and my ticket. I kissed them both. The twenty-dollar bill was stuck in the passport. It had been an inexpensive holiday. I had a real moment of conflict regarding the vanity case, but in the end, I decided I could live without it.

"I'm ready," I said.

"This is crazy." She tilted her face toward the only window in the room.

"I said I'm ready," I stated as I dragged the case along the brick floor of the patio. Fatima almost had a fit to see me involved in such exertion. She snatched the case from me. The chauffeur waiting at the big portals took the case from her, and I gave Fatima a good-bye squeeze that embarrassed both of us.

Joanne was running toward me, holding Abbas by the hand. "Abbas," I said, and I kissed him a dozen times, "you've been a real pal." Then I made the dash down the steps, Joanne in hot pursuit.

There was a nifty gray Mercedes parked in the clearing next to the yellow Land-Rover, and the chauffeur stored my valise in its sleek trunk.

"Well, so long," I said.

She gave me this look as if I were abandoning her. As though she'd returned on my account. I didn't know which I wanted more, to get into the car or begin pushing it toward Hetron. "It'll be all right, Joanne. You'll have these kids . . . raise a couple of allies . . . things change."

"And what about you, Hope?" She was still not letting me leave. "What are you going back to?"

"Well, lately, I've been giving a lot of thought to the computer field," I admitted. I slid into the leather embrace of the Mercedes, and we were rolling. I swiveled around to get a rear-

window view, and as the scene receded, I memorized it all—
Joanne with Abbas hoisted in her arms at ground level, above
them the palace, almost hidden by trees and walls. And above it
all, at the upper edge of the frame, a movement, a form, making its way down a rocky path.

A NOTE ON THE TYPE

The text of this book was set in film in a type
face known as Garamond. The design is based
on letter forms originally created by Claude
Garamond (c. 1480–1561). Garamond was a
pupil of Geoffroy Tory and may have patterned
his letter forms on Venetian models. To this
day, the type face that bears his name is one of
the most attractive used in book composition,
and the intervening years have caused it to lose
little of its freshness or beauty.

Composed by American–Stratford
Graphic Services, Inc.,
Brattleboro, Vermont

Printed and bound by
Fairfield Graphics
Fairfield, Pennsylvania

Design by Judy Henry